Mandy went down the corridor and out of the hospital's main doors. She was just about to cross the car park, when she stopped dead.

A small brown-and-white Jack Russell terrier was standing a short distance away, watching her.

'Hello,' she said gently. 'What are you doing here, all on your own?'

The little dog whined softly. But although it wagged its long, undocked tail, it didn't come any nearer.

The little dog looked at her with intelligent brown eyes, but stood its ground. Then its ears twitched and for a moment, Mandy's spirits lifted. It was going to come to her!

But, suddenly, the dog gave another soft whine, then turned and dashed away into some shrubs.

LUCY DANIELS

Terrier
— in the —
Tinsel

Illustrations by Ann Baum

Hodder
Children's
Books

a division of Hodder Headline Limited

Special thanks to Sue Bentley

Animal Ark is a trademark of Working Partners Limited
Text copyright © 2001 Working Partners Limited
Created by Working Partners Limited, London W6 0QT
Original series created by Ben M. Baglio
Illustrations copyright © 2001 Ann Baum

First published in Great Britain in 2001
by Hodder Children's Books

For more information about Animal Ark,
please contact www.animalark.co.uk

10 9 8 7 6 5

A Catalogue record for this book is available from the British Library

ISBN 0 340 79556 5

Typeset by Avon Dataset Ltd, Bidford-on-Avon, Warks

Printed and bound in Great Britain by
Clays Ltd, St Ives plc

Hodder Children's Books
a division of Hodder Headline Limited
338 Euston Road
London NW1 3BH

One

Mandy Hope walked into the kitchen at Animal Ark. 'Dad, what on earth are you doing?' she said, trying not to laugh.

'Hello, love.' Adam Hope smiled as he struggled into the bright red jacket of a Santa suit. 'I'm just trying on my costume for the grotto at Walton Cottage Hospital,' he explained.

'Looks to me like it's not going to do up! Perhaps you should have tried it on before lunch!' Mandy said. 'Here, let me help you.' She pulled the sides of the jacket together and fastened the buttons. The material strained under the pressure.

'Thanks, love,' Adam Hope said with a grin.

'I'm sure this suit must have shrunk when your mum washed it.'

'Hmm.' Mandy wasn't convinced. 'Maybe you should have stuck to your diet!' She laughed.

Mr Hope flexed his shoulders and looked down at himself. 'Nope, this is fine,' he insisted. 'I'll look just the part.' He took off the jacket and hung it on the back of the kitchen door.

'Well, you'll certainly be a perfect Santa, with your round tummy,' Mandy teased.

'Cheek! Phew, I think we need a cup of tea after that,' her dad announced, with an amused gleam in his eye. 'I'll make one for your mum too, she's just finishing up in the operating theatre.'

Mandy remembered that this morning her mum had been operating on Peaches, an elderly guinea-pig. Peaches was lovely, with rosettes of creamy fur. She belonged to seven-year-old Laura, who lived near Mandy's best friend, James Hunter.

Emily Hope came into the kitchen just as her husband was filling the kettle. She smiled when she saw Mandy. 'No more school till next year!' she joked.

Mandy nodded. 'Yup! And I can't wait for Christmas Day. Only four days to go! How's Peaches?'

'She's only just come round from the anaesthetic,' said Mrs Hope. 'She's still quite groggy. I had to remove a very large bladder stone.'

'But she is going to pull through, isn't she?' Mandy said worriedly. She knew how much Laura loved her pet.

'It's too early to say, love,' her mum replied, looking serious. She ran a hand through her long red hair. 'Peaches is stable at the moment, but we have to remember that she's quite old.'

Mandy nodded. She knew that an operation placed a serious strain on any animal – even more if they were getting old. It looked like the next few days were going to be touch and go for poor Peaches.

'Maybe Mandy could keep an eye on Peaches?' Adam Hope suggested.

Mandy brightened. She felt better knowing that there was something she could do. 'What's that stuff that causes bladder stones? Ox-something, acid, isn't it?' she asked.

'That's right. Oxalic acid,' her mum replied.

'Caused by feeding too many brassicas,' Mr Hope said. He handed Mandy and her mum a mug of tea each.

'What are brassicas?' Mandy asked, taking a cautious sip of the hot tea.

'It's the name for all the plants of the cabbage family,' Mrs Hope explained. 'Like kale, cauliflower and spinach. Too much of that kind of food can upset certain guinea-pigs.'

'So will Peaches need to be put on a special diet when she's better?' Mandy asked.

'Yes. She'll probably do better if she sticks to grass, hay and grain, with fruit and veg in small amounts,' Mrs Hope said. 'I'll have a chat with Laura and her mum about it when they call in.'

Mandy took her drink over to the window and saw James stepping out of his father's car. 'Here's James,' she said. 'I'd better go and get ready. We're going over to Lilac Cottage. Gran and Grandad will be waiting for us.'

'Oh, you're helping to decorate my grotto at Walton Hospital this afternoon, aren't you?' her dad remembered. 'Tell your gran that the Santa suit is a perfect fit. And Santa is polishing his boots and grooming his reindeer!'

'Da-ad!' Mandy put her empty mug in the sink and headed for the stairs.

* * *

It was cold and frosty in the pale afternoon sun and Mandy and James's breath steamed in the air as they walked along the lane. Behind the hedgerows, the fields were bare and bleak.

James lifted his head and sniffed the cold air. 'My dad reckons he can smell snow in the air. But I can't!'

'Me neither,' Mandy said. 'I wish it *would* snow. I'd really love a white Christmas.'

'Yeah!' James agreed. 'Snowball fights and sledging and snowboarding. Blackie loves going for walks in the snow too.' Blackie was James's pet Labrador.

'Blackie loves walks full stop!' Mandy said.

James grinned and pushed his glasses up to the bridge of his nose. 'He's getting better about walking on a lead, you know,' he said proudly. 'And he actually came when I called him yesterday.'

'Wonders will never cease!' Mandy said affectionately. Blackie was lovely, but he wasn't exactly obedient.

They had almost reached Lilac Cottage. 'Oh, look,' Mandy said, waving. 'There's Grandad on the drive. He's loading up the camper van.'

Grandad waved back. 'Hello, you two!' he called out as Mandy and James stopped to open the garden gate. 'I'm glad you're here. Just look at this lot!'

Mandy saw that a pile of wood and some boards were already stacked inside the back of the van. 'Are we going to need all that, Grandad?' She asked.

'Oh, yes. We have to make the grotto first, then we decorate it,' her grandad replied.

Dorothy Hope came out of the cottage, her arms full of more props. 'Hello, Mandy, love. Hello, James,' she called out, peering at them from behind the pile of boxes she was carrying. 'This lot isn't the half of it!' Suddenly the boxes began to slip sideways. 'Oops,' Gran gasped.

James dashed over to help. 'I've got them!' he said, steadying the load.

'Oh, thank you, dear,' Mrs Hope said gratefully. 'There's more boxes in the hallway if you two could fetch them for me.'

Mandy and James helped load all the boxes, which were bulging with decorations, into the van. It was a squeeze to get the back door locked, but Grandad finally managed it.

'Phew!' James said.

Grandad chuckled. 'Mrs Ponsonby has been collecting donations of props and decorations for the grotto,' he explained. 'I've never seen so much tinsel in my life!'

'Mrs Ponsonby can be very . . . enthusiastic!' Gran opened the door and got into the driving seat.

'Enthusiastic? That's one word for it,' Grandad murmured.

Mandy and James laughed. Mrs Ponsonby was the bossiest woman in Welford.

'I bet no one dared to refuse her!' Mandy said.

They set off through the village and took the winding road that led across the moors to Walton. Gran turned on the radio and a woman's voice filled the van. 'So come along one and all and bring your gifts to Walton Cottage Hospital . . .'

'Listen! It's the local radio station's Christmas appeal,' Mandy said.

'That's right,' said James. 'People are being asked to buy an extra Christmas present for the children who will be in hospital over Christmas. My mum bought one last week.'

'Did she? Well, it's for a very good cause,' Gran said. 'We're going to put a collection bin for the gifts in the grotto. Then Santa will give them out on Christmas Eve.'

'Local children can visit Santa in the grotto

too,' Grandad added. 'We're going to charge them fifty pence per visit and donate all the money to the hospital.'

Mandy thought that was a great idea.

The stone cottages and farm buildings on the high moors sped past, and soon Gran was turning into the hospital car park. She pulled into an empty space near the entrance and turned off the engine. 'Right, let's go and find out where we're supposed to be setting up,' she said.

'I'll go and ask,' Grandad volunteered. He undid his seatbelt and climbed out of the van. 'Won't be a tick,' he said, walking off.

'Shall we start getting the stuff out, Gran?' Mandy offered.

'Good idea, Mandy,' Gran nodded.

By the time Tom Hope returned, they had most of the boxes and all of the wood stacked in the car park. 'I hadn't realised quite how much stuff we had,' he chuckled, eyeing the impressive pile. 'We're in a side room, just along the corridor from the children's ward. Straight through the main doors and turn right,' he said.

'OK.' Mandy and James sprang into action, each grabbing a box of decorations.

They were just returning to the van for a second load when a hospital porter came out of the hospital. 'Hi! I saw you struggling. Need an extra hand?' he asked.

'Oh, thanks,' Mandy and James said gratefully.

'No problem,' the porter replied with a friendly grin, shouldering some lengths of wood.

In the side room, they found Gran standing with her hands on her hips. Mandy saw that she was looking worriedly at the floor which was fast disappearing beneath all the material for the grotto.

'Oh dear. It's looking a bit chaotic,' Gran said, surveying the mess.

'Perhaps we could make a start and leave the rest outside for later?' Mandy suggested.

'That's a good idea,' James agreed.

'If there's nothing else to bring in for the moment, I'll get back to work then,' the porter said cheerily. 'Bye. Have fun!'

'Thanks for your help!' Mandy called after him.

'Er . . . I suppose there is a plan, Dorothy?' Tom Hope said to his wife.

'Oh, yes, Where's that drawing I made . . .' Gran produced a piece of paper from her trouser pocket. 'Here it is.' She smoothed it out and laid it on a table at the side of the room.

Mandy, James and Grandad studied Gran's drawing. Then they turned back and looked at all the material for the grotto.

'What are those panel things?' James asked.

'Those are display boards,' Gran said. 'From a shop that was closing down. Mrs Ponsonby went in and asked if we could have them as they were just going to throw them away.'

'Good for her!' Mandy whispered to James.

Grandad frowned. 'Display boards? They look a bit complicated to me.'

'It's quite simple to put them together,' Gran said confidently. 'Mandy and James can help me sort out all the bits. Why don't you fetch your toolbox? We'll need screws and a screwdriver.'

'Right you are,' said Grandad, looking a bit happier now that he knew what had to be done. He set off down the corridor, whistling under his breath.

'Your gran's a brilliant organiser,' James whispered.

Mandy grinned. 'I know!'

Half an hour later, everything had begun to take shape. The wooden frames for the display boards had been fastened together. Now Mandy, James and Gran were steadying the panels, while Grandad slotted them into place.

Mandy caught a movement out of the corner of her eye and looked up. She saw a fair-haired boy peering at them curiously. He looked about nine years old and was wearing a tartan dressing-gown over bright yellow pyjamas.

Mandy smiled at him and he flashed her a cheeky grin before wandering away.

'Well, what do you think, Dorothy?' Grandad tightened the final screw.

They all stood back and looked at the display units. There were five of them, each about a metre and a half tall.

'They aren't going to fall over on anybody, are they?' Gran asked, sounding worried.

Grandad puffed out his chest. 'Steady as a rock, these are.'

'Gran's just teasing,' Mandy said. 'I think they're brilliant. Don't you, James?'

'Definitely,' James agreed.

Grandad looked pleased. He turned to his wife. 'They'll need sprucing up a bit. The fabric covering the boards is very shabby.'

'Don't worry,' said Gran. 'I've got lots of silver paper which will be just the job.'

'What are those for?' asked a voice behind Mandy and James.

Mandy turned around. It was the boy who had been watching them earlier. He stood in the doorway, an interested expression on his round face.

'Hi,' said Mandy. 'We're building a Christmas grotto. I'm Mandy and this is James,' she added. 'And that's my gran and grandad over there. What's your name?'

'Charlie,' the little boy replied. 'What's the grotto for?'

Mandy explained that it was so that local children could visit Santa.

'And children in hospital, like you, can come here too or Santa will visit them in the ward,' James put in.

Charlie put his head on one side as if he was thinking about this. 'I don't need Santa to visit me in bed. I've had bronchitis, but I'm nearly better now.'

'Oh, that's good,' Mandy said. 'So you should be going home for Christmas?'

Charlie nodded. 'I can't wait. There's not much to do around here. It's dead boring.'

'We're just about to start covering the display

boards with silver paper. Would you like to help us?' Mandy suggested.

'Cool!' Charlie's blue eyes lit up and he nodded eagerly. He began rummaging about in the nearest box.

While Mandy and James dragged the display boards into position, Charlie pulled out rolls of silver foil and coloured paper. He heaped them all together on the floor along with silver streamers and stars, then went to fetch the rest of the boxes from the corridor.

James was searching for a roll of sticky tape, when Charlie suddenly burst through the door and barged into him.

'Ooh, sorry,' Charlie said apologetically, his arms round a large box.

'That's OK.' James rubbed his bruised ankle.

Mandy gave him a sympathetic look. 'Have you got some sticky tape in your toolbox, Grandad?' she asked, turning to Tom Hope.

'I'm sure I have. Oh, that's funny.' Grandad scratched his head, looking puzzled. 'Where *is* my toolbox. It was here just a minute ago . . .'

'It can't be far away, Tom,' Gran said. 'You only just had it.'

Mandy and James started looking for the

toolbox. But after a couple of minutes they had still found no sign of it.

'That's weird,' James said, pushing back his floppy fringe. 'Maybe it's been covered up by something.'

He began looking under the coils of streamers and moving empty cardboard boxes. Mandy helped him, but had no luck.

'Found it!' Charlie suddenly called out triumphantly. 'It was under all this tinsel stuff! Sorry!'

'Mystery solved!' Grandad said with a grin. He threw the roll of tape across to James.

James caught it. 'I don't know if Charlie's helping or getting in the way . . .' he whispered to Mandy.

'Well, at least he seems to be enjoying himself!' she said with a grin.

'Charlie Kingston!' called a cheery voice from the corridor. Then a nurse popped her head into the room. 'Ah, there you are. Your tea's ready in the ward.'

Charlie screwed up his nose. 'I don't want any. I want to stay here and help.'

'Did someone say tea?' Grandad said hopefully.

The nurse smiled at him. 'I'll see what can be

arranged. It's the least we can do for our volunteers! Come along, Charlie, you need to eat something.'

'Can't I help with the grotto?' Charlie pleaded, his expression downcast.

'You can come back and help later, Charlie,' the nurse said.

'We're going to be here for ages yet, aren't we, Gran?' Mandy joined in, seeing Charlie's disappointed face.

'Oh, yes. Probably tomorrow too,' Gran agreed.

'OK.' Charlie's face brightened up. 'I suppose I *am* a bit hungry,' he said, following the nurse out of the room.

'He's really keen to help, isn't he?' James said. 'Imagine wanting to miss out on your tea!'

'Can't understand that at all!' Mandy replied innocently, opening her eyes wide. James was famous for his healthy appetite.

James went a bit pink and grinned at Mandy.

'Here's our tea now,' Grandad said, as a nurse came into the room carrying a tray with four cups and a plate of biscuits on it. 'Thanks. Custard creams, my favourite.'

James and Mandy perched on the side table and helped themselves.

'I think I'll just pop along to see Percy Green in Ward Twelve before we get going again,' Gran said when she had finished her cup of tea.

'Who's Percy Green?' asked Mandy.

'A recent addition to your gran's Meals-on-Wheels round,' Grandad said. 'The old gentleman was brought in yesterday after a bad asthma attack, wasn't he, Dorothy?'

Gran nodded. 'That's right. He collapsed in his garden. Luckily a neighbour found him and called an ambulance. I'd just like to check up on him.'

'I'll come with you,' Mandy offered.

'All right,' said Gran. 'You can help me cheer Percy up. I haven't known him all that long, but I'm sure he'd like some visitors.'

Ward Twelve was just down the corridor. It was a bright airy room, made cheerful by the vases of flowers beside most of the beds. Gran checked with the nurse that it was all right to visit Percy.

'You go ahead,' the nurse said. 'Mr Green might enjoy a visit. He's a bit tired and unsettled. A friendly face always helps.'

Mandy and Gran smiled and said good afternoon to some of the patients who were reading or listening to the radio through earphones. At the end of the ward, Mandy spotted a man lying in a bed. He seemed to be asleep and looked pale and rather thin.

'That's Percy,' Gran said.

As Mandy and Gran reached his bedside, Percy stirred and opened his eyes.

'Hello, Percy,' Gran said gently. 'How are you feeling?'

The old man looked up and raised his head. His faded blue eyes flickered over them.

'Where ... Where is he?' Percy muttered, his forehead creasing with worry. 'Not ... here ...'

'Where's who, dear?' Gran said leaning forward. 'Who's not here?'

But Percy had sunk back on to the pillows. His lips moved, but he had closed his eyes again. His words came out in a whisper. 'He's not here ... where is he ...?'

'Oh, dear.' Gran looked worried. 'I think he must be asking about his son.'

She turned to Mandy and explained quietly that Percy had lived with his son and his family. 'But then his son received a very good offer of work in America, so he's taken his family to live out there for a year. Percy could have gone with them, but he wanted to stay on in the family house in Welford.'

'So Percy lives on his own now?' Mandy said, feeling concerned.

Gran nodded. 'That's why I wanted to pop in and check on him. Come on, love. I think Percy's gone back to sleep. Let's leave him to rest. It's the best thing for him. We can come back another time.'

'OK,' Mandy said. 'I'll come with you next time.' As she left Ward Twelve and went back towards the room where the grotto was going to be, she couldn't help feeling worried about the confused old man.

Two

'That silver foil looks really good!' Mandy and Gran came back to find James and Grandad hard at work.

'It's supposed to look like the walls of an ice cave.' James explained. 'At least, it will do when it's finished.'

'How was Percy?' Grandad asked.

'He seemed a bit mixed up, didn't he, Gran?' Mandy said.

Gran nodded. 'Poor old chap. I expect he's still a bit shaken up by being poorly.'

'Gran and I are going to see him again tomorrow,' Mandy said.

'Good idea,' Grandad agreed. 'He might be feeling better by then.'

James waved Mandy over to help him cover the next board. Mandy held the foil as James stuck it down. They managed to cover half of another board before the foil ran out.

'There's loads more in the van. I'll go and get some,' Mandy offered. She went down the corridor and out of the main doors. She was just about to cross the car park, when she stopped dead.

A small brown-and-white Jack Russell terrier was standing a short distance away, watching her.

As soon as Mandy took a step towards it, the little dog backed away. Mandy stopped and crouched down. She knew that if she made herself look smaller, it would seem less threatening to the dog.

'Hello,' she said gently. 'What are you doing here, all on your own?'

The little dog whined softly. But although it wagged its long, undocked tail, it didn't come any nearer.

Mandy thought it seemed quite nervous. 'I wonder who you belong to,' she said softly. She looked around, but could see no sign of an owner.

The terrier looked well fed and was wearing a collar. Mandy didn't think it could be a stray.

She tried again, speaking in a coaxing voice and rubbing the tips of her fingers together encouragingly. 'Come here. It's all right. I won't hurt you.'

The little dog looked at her with intelligent brown eyes, but stood its ground. Its ears twitched and, for a moment, Mandy's spirits lifted. It was going to come to her!

Suddenly, the dog gave another soft whine, then turned and dashed away into some shrubs.

Mandy felt a stab of disappointment. She stared after the dog, but it had disappeared into the shadows.

'Oh, it's that Jack Russell again,' said a voice at her elbow.

Mandy turned to see the porter who had helped them unload the van earlier. 'Hello,' she said. 'So you've seen it here before, have you? Do you know who it belongs to?'

The porter shook his head. 'It's been hanging around for a couple of days. I've tried to catch it and so have a couple of other people but it won't let anyone near it. I'm not surprised that it's a bit nervous, though. The poor little thing was almost hit by an ambulance,' he explained. 'One of the guards told me he saw it run straight in front of it. The dog had a lucky escape.'

'Oh no!' Mandy gasped. 'No wonder it's scared.' She felt worried about the Jack Russell. Someone must be missing it. And it had been around for a couple of days. What was it eating? And where could it be sleeping?

'You seemed to know what you were doing just then,' the porter said. 'For a minute, I thought the dog was going to come to you.'

Mandy smiled. 'I love animals. My Mum and Dad are vets in Welford. I often help out in their surgery.'

'Ah. That explains it,' he said. 'Well, I'd better go. I've got a patient to take down to X-ray.'

'OK,' Mandy said, 'I'm going to have a quick look round the grounds. I might be able to find the dog.'

'Best of luck then,' the porter said. 'Let me know how you get on.'

'OK, I will. Thanks.' Mandy smiled and set off towards the shrubs where the terrier had disappeared.

Ten minutes later, she had searched behind all

the bushes on the narrow strip of lawn at the edge of the car park, and now she was looking underneath every parked car.

The light was fading fast and it would soon be dark. There was no time to do a more complete search, so Mandy decided to head straight for the place outside the hospital canteen where the waste bins were kept. If the dog was a stray, then maybe it would be hanging around there looking for food. But, again, she found nothing.

The Jack Russell was still on her mind when she went back to James and her grandparents.

'Haven't you got it?' James glanced at her empty hands. 'You've been ages.'

'Got what?' Mandy looked blank.

'The tinfoil. Remember?' he said.

'Oh!' Mandy's hands flew to her mouth. 'I completely forgot! Sorry.'

'What have you been doing all this time?' Gran asked suspiciously.

Mandy gave an embarrassed grin. 'There was a Jack Russell outside, all by itself. I tried to get close to it, but it ran off. The porter said it had been here for a couple of days. Maybe it's a stray after all . . .' she finished thoughtfully.

'Did you look for it?' James asked. He seemed

to have forgotten all about tinfoil now.

Mandy nodded. 'I looked round the car park, but there was no sign of it.'

Gran shook her head. 'You and animals, Mandy Hope! And James is almost as bad!' She chuckled. 'I expect that little dog's all tucked up in front of a cosy fire by now!'

Mandy remembered how well cared for the dog had looked, and thought that her Gran was probably right.

'Which dog?' said a familiar voice. It was Charlie again, his bright blue eyes wide with curiosity. 'Is it yours, Mandy?'

'No,' Mandy said. 'I don't have any pets of my own. Dad says that we've got enough to do without looking after everyone else's animals!'

'Mandy's parents are both vets,' James explained.

'Cool!' Charlie said. 'So you get to share everyone else's pets!'

Mandy smiled at Charlie's eager face. 'I suppose I do.'

'Whose dog are you talking about?' Charlie wanted to know.

Mandy told him about the Jack Russell which had narrowly escaped being hit by an ambulance.

'I searched for it, but it disappeared. I think it went back to its owner,' she finished, sounding more sure than she felt.

Charlie's face lit up. 'I love Jack Russells,' he announced. 'They're dead cheeky!' But then he frowned. 'I hope it *has* gone home. I've just been watching TV. The weatherman says it's going to snow tonight.'

Mandy glanced across at James. She hated to think that there was a chance of the little dog spending the night outdoors.

'And talking about cosy fires . . .' Grandad prompted.

Gran took the hint. 'Time to pack up and go home, I think.'

'Oh. You said I could help you again!' Charlie protested. He seemed to be bursting with energy.

'Course you can,' Mandy said. 'You can help us tidy up, then we'll be back tomorrow to do the interesting bit – decorating the grotto.'

'OK.' Charlie began throwing things back into boxes. 'I'll come back then.'

'Phew!' James whistled under his breath. 'He's a real live wire, isn't he?'

But Mandy didn't hear him. She had a picture in her mind of a little brown-and-white dog with a sweet face. It was huddled in the shadows, shivering with cold while thick snow fell all around.

'Bye, Mandy. Have a good Christmas!' Simon, the practice nurse at Animal Ark, was crunching across the frosty gravel towards his car when Mandy arrived back home.

'Bye, Simon! You too!' Mandy called. She waved as Simon drove out on to the lane. He was off to stay with his mum and dad.

Mandy went straight through the cottage and into the modern extension at the back, which housed her parents' surgery. The waiting-room was crammed to bursting point with sick pets and their owners, eager to be seen before the Christmas holiday. Through the open door of one of the treatment rooms, Mandy glimpsed her dad lifting a pet carrier on to the table.

'If you'd like to take Tina in now.' Jean Knox, the grey-haired receptionist, sent in Emily Hope's next patient, a kitten here for a routine injection.

Mandy took one look at the line of people waiting at the desk then asked Jean, 'What needs doing?'

'Oh, thanks, Mandy dear.' Jean looked even

more flustered than usual. She fumbled for her glasses that usually hung on a chain round her neck.

'On top of your head,' Mandy whispered.

'Of course, thanks, dear.' Jean pulled her glasses down to her nose. 'Could you get this patient some worming tablets, please? And this lady needs some medicated shampoo for her poodle.'

Mandy helped behind the desk for the next twenty minutes. She checked appointment details on the computer, and handed out shampoo and worming tablets to people who didn't need to see her mum or dad.

'Oh good, you're back, Mandy!' Emily Hope poked her head round the door of the second treatment room. 'I need another pair of hands. Can you spare her, Jean?'

Jean said she could manage now, so Mandy went to help her mum. There was a huge grey rabbit on the treatment table. 'Wow! It's enormous. What sort is it?' she asked, unhooking a white coat from behind the door and putting it on.

'A Flemish giant,' her mum answered. 'And they're very strong. Hold him still, would you, love?' Mrs Hope bent close as she cleaned the rabbit's cut foot. 'How's the grotto coming along?'

'Fine.' Mandy cradled the rabbit in both arms, holding it so that it didn't struggle. The rabbit's owner, a serious-faced boy of about ten, watched her with his dad.

'We've had a boy called Charlie helping us,' she told her mum.

Emily Hope threw a used cottonwool pad into the bin and reached for a box of antibiotic powder. 'So, do you think you'll finish it tomorrow? Your dad's keen to see his grotto!'

'Mmm. Should do . . .' Mandy murmured. The Jack Russell was still on her mind.

Her mum looked up and narrowed her eyes. 'Out with it,' she ordered kindly.

'Out with what?' Mandy blinked at her.

'Whatever's bothering you,' Mrs Hope replied.

Mandy grinned. 'Well – there was this sweet little dog at the hospital. I thought that he might be a stray . . .' She repeated the saga of the Jack Russell yet again. 'So – what do you think?' she asked when she'd finished.

Her mum shrugged thoughtfully. 'I'd say that your gran's probably right about the dog going home. But we'll talk about it later, when it's less busy, if you like. OK?'

'OK,' Mandy agreed. 'It's mad out there.

Everyone in Welford seems to have brought their pet in for something!'

After the huge rabbit, Mandy helped her mum treat a cat with a gashed face and a Border collie with an eye infection. Then Jean needed more help in Reception.

Surgery was almost over and Mandy was back in the treatment room, getting ready to wipe down the examination table, when the door opened. A rather stout lady in a tweed suit sailed in. It was Mrs Ponsonby. Pandora, her pet Pekinese, was tucked under one arm and Toby, her scruffy mongrel pup, trotted beside her on a lead.

'Oh, no. I wonder what's wrong this time?' Mandy whispered to her mum. Probably the old lady's portly Pekinese had refused its tenth juicy treat or snuffled a bit too loudly. Pandora had to be the most spoiled pet in Welford!

'Hello, Mrs Ponsonby,' Mrs Hope said cheerfully, tucking a few strands of hair behind her ear. 'What's the matter with Pandora?'

'Oh, Pandora's fine. Just darling, as usual!' Mrs Ponsonby's bossy voice filled the room. 'It's Toby I've come about.'

'Oh, right.' Mrs Hope raised her eyebrows at Mandy. 'Let's have him up on the table then,

Mandy. What's the problem, Mrs Ponsonby?'

'Well.' The old lady pursed her lips in annoyance. 'I was outside the Post Office, posting a Christmas card, when a rude young man came dashing out of the shop. He just pushed straight past me! Toby gave a yelp, and I realised that the brute had trodden on his foot.'

'Oh, poor you.' Mandy stroked the little mongrel's head. Toby yapped sharply and reached up to lick her chin. His tail was wagging madly.

'I'd have given that young man what for!' Mrs Ponsonby went on fiercely. 'But he had already roared off in one of those flashy fast cars.'

Luckily for him, Mandy thought. Mrs Ponsonby would have made mincemeat out of him.

'Well, Toby doesn't seem too distressed,' said Emily Hope. 'Which paw was it? I'll just check him over.'

While Mandy soothed the wriggling dog, her mum ran expert fingers over his sore foot. Pandora looked on untroubled from Mrs Ponsonby's arms. Her long creamy fur flowed over her owner's coat sleeve.

'There's some swelling, but it's not serious. I think the foot's just bruised,' Mrs Hope decided.

Toby wriggled and nudged Mandy's chin with his cold wet nose.

'There's not much wrong with you, is there?' Mandy tickled his warm chest.

'I'd like to see him moving about. Could you put him on the floor, please, Mandy?' Mrs Hope asked.

Toby trotted around, sniffing the floor and poking into the corners of the room. Mrs Hope watched closely. At last she gave a satisfied nod. 'He seems to be bearing his weight on that foot. I don't think we need to X-ray it.'

'Oh, thank heavens he's all right!' Mrs Ponsonby bent over and scratched the top of her dog's rough little head. 'Let's take you home, Toby dear, and find you a special treat.'

Mandy rolled her eyes. If Toby wasn't careful he was going to end up as portly as Pandora.

'Not too many treats,' Mrs Hope advised.

Mrs Ponsonby didn't seem to hear. 'Thank you so much, Emily,' she said cheerily, picking up Toby's lead and heading for the door. 'I'll see you tomorrow, Mandy,' she called over her shoulder. 'I'm going to pop along to see how the grotto's turned out.'

'That's all we need.' Mandy groaned as Mrs

Ponsonby closed the door behind her.

Emily Hope chuckled and gave her a hug. 'Whatever you say about that woman, you have to admit that she loves those dogs!' She led the way out into the reception room where Jean was just putting on her coat.

'Bye, Jean. See you tomorrow.' Mandy waved goodbye and locked the surgery door behind her before joining her parents in the kitchen.

'Supper!' Mr Hope peeled off his white vet's coat and hung it on the back of the kitchen door. 'What I wouldn't give for a poached egg on toast!' he groaned.

'Double pocket money this week?' Mandy suggested with a chuckle.

Adam Hope pulled a face. 'Nice try!'

Mrs Hope joined in the laughter. 'You two make a great double act!' She went over to the sink to fill the kettle. 'Everyone for a cup of tea?'

'I've just got to go and see Peaches first,' Mandy said. She went back through the surgery and into the residential unit where animals that were too sick to go home were kept. Rows of wire cages filled the room, which was spotlessly clean. Mandy went past each one, checking that the patients all had clean water and bedding.

Peaches was curled up on a pile of straw. Mandy could see her shaved side and the neatly stitched operation wound. She put her face close to the cage and looked in. Peaches's pink nose twitched and she opened her gentle brown eyes.

'Oh, good. You're awake,' Mandy said softly. 'Aren't you beautiful?'

Laura had told her that Peaches was an Abyssinian – a rough-haired breed. The creamy coat grew in rosettes all over Peaches's body, making her fur stand up in all directions.

Mandy put a finger inside the cage to stroke the guinea-pig. 'I wonder if you're hungry?' She went to the fridge and cut a small chunk of cucumber. Peaches could eat this safely as it wasn't leafy and cabbagey. Mandy opened the cage and put the morsel inside.

Peaches's pink nose twitched more rapidly. She leaned forwards and butted the juicy treat, but didn't touch it. Mandy noticed that she was still quite wobbly. She hoped that it was just the after-effects of the anaesthetic. 'Now you just get better, Peaches,' she said in a soft voice. 'And then Laura will come and take you home.'

Peaches turned to look at her. She twitched her pink nose and gave a warbling chirrup. Then she turned her back on the cucumber and burrowed down into her clean straw.

'Have a good rest. I'll come and see you again tomorrow.' Mandy was still worried about the guinea-pig. Peaches seemed to be getting better, but she wouldn't regain her strength if she didn't eat something soon.

Three

Saturday morning dawned cold and crisp. Mandy looked out of her bedroom window at the frost-covered grass. No sign of snow yet. She pulled on a warm jumper and her jeans, then dashed downstairs.

Adam Hope was ironing his white vet's coat in the kitchen. He looked up and smiled. 'You seem in a hurry!'

'I am!' Mandy said. 'I'm meeting James. We're taking the bus over to Walton and meeting Gran and Grandad at the hospital.'

'Well, make time for breakfast,' her dad said, wagging his finger jokingly. 'It's the most important meal of the day.'

'Yes, Dad!' Mandy rolled her eyes. Then she saw the pan on the cooker. 'Oh, great. Porridge!' She helped herself to a steaming bowlful.

Mandy blew on each spoonful as she ate it. A few minutes later, she jumped up from the table and rinsed the empty bowl in the sink. 'Got to go!'

Mr Hope was just slipping on his coat, ready for morning surgery. Mandy kissed his cheek. 'See you later!'

As Mandy walked towards the Fox and Goose crossroads, she saw James already waiting there. He had a holdall slung over one shoulder.

'Hurry up!' he shouted, waving frantically. 'There's a bus just coming.'

Mandy sped up and arrived, out of breath, just as the bus pulled up. 'We're going to be really early for meeting Gran and Grandad,' she said.

'Not if we call into the pet shop,' James said promptly, getting on to the bus.

'Why would we want to do that?' Mandy threw him a puzzled look as she paid for a ticket. 'Apart from looking at all the brilliant animals.'

'Which you'd just hate, of course!' James joked.

'I want to buy a Christmas stocking for Blackie. They've got some really good ones.'

'OK!' Mandy took a seat next to James as the bus set off through Welford village.

Twenty minutes later, they were opening the pet shop door. Mandy loved the rich smell of animal food and straw that greeted them as they went inside.

'Wow!' James looked wide-eyed at the display of Christmas gifts for animals. There were edible treats for every pet from budgies and hamsters to cats and dogs. On one rack there were also toys – balls with bells inside, catnip mice and plastic balls that dispensed treats as they were rolled about.

'And look at these squeaky dog-pulls and new leads!' Mandy said.

'Yeah, they're great. But there's too much choice.' James fiddled with his glasses and groaned. 'I can't decide what to get now.'

'No contest.' Mandy tilted her head. 'A stocking, definitely! Otherwise, how will Blackie know it's Christmas?'

James laughed and reached up for the biggest doggie stocking on the shelf. 'Blackie's going to love this. He won't be able to move for a week once he's eaten all these treats,' he said, as he went over to pay.

Mandy raised her eyebrows. Blackie keeping still, and not demanding a walk? Not likely!

With the stocking safely stowed in James's holdall, Mandy and James walked along the road to the hospital.

'Look, there's Gran and Grandad's van,' Mandy said, pointing across the car park.

As they approached the main door, a small brown-and-white dog came out from behind some bushes. It stopped when it saw them and hung back warily.

Mandy froze. 'Look!' she whispered. 'It's that Jack Russell again.'

James stopped dead too. He frowned. 'Do you think it's been here all night?'

'It must be cold and hungry if it has,' Mandy said worriedly. 'I'm going to see if I can make friends with it.'

She moved forward very slowly, careful to avoid direct eye contact with the little dog. 'Hello again. Don't be afraid,' she said soothingly.

The Jack Russell gave a soft whine and licked its lip nervously. It pattered sideways on its short legs, but didn't run away. The metal disc on its collar jingled as it moved. Mandy peered at the disc, but she couldn't make out what it said.

'I think it wants to be friends,' James said in a low voice. 'But it seems very timid.'

The Jack Russell dipped its head and it took a few steps forward. It whined softly.

Mandy held her breath. 'That's it. Come here,' she encouraged gently.

The dog blinked at her and moved closer still. Slowly, Mandy stretched out her hand and let the dog sniff it. A moment later, she felt a wet cold nose brush against her fingers.

'Good boy!' Mandy tickled the dog's white chest.

'Well done, Mandy,' James whispered behind her.

'Isn't he lovely?' The Jack Russell had half closed its eyes and Mandy risked stroking its soft ears. She was just reaching out her fingers to take hold of its collar when the little dog darted sideways and took off across the car park. 'Oh no.' Mandy's spirits sank. Just when she was getting somewhere!

She turned round to look at James. Over his shoulder she saw a security guard coming towards them. He must have startled the dog.

The guard wore a broad grin. 'You're the first

person who's got anywhere near that little crafty beggar!'

'Crafty?' Mandy echoed, puzzled. 'Why? What's he done?'

'Swiped a bag of crisps earlier on, that's what!'

'Were they yours?' James asked.

The guard shook his head. 'A little girl dropped them as she was getting into a car. And that terrier popped out of the bushes, grabbed the bag, and took off. He's quite a character.'

'Do you know who he belongs to?' Mandy asked.

'No. But I've seen him around here for a couple of days now.' The guard shrugged and headed back to his cabin at the entrance of the car park.

'That's just what the porter said, isn't it?' James commented as they went in to meet her grandparents.

'Yes,' Mandy agreed feeling even more worried. 'Do you think it's a stray?'

'Could be.' James looked thoughtful. 'We could ask around and see if any other people have seen it.'

'Good idea,' Mandy said. 'At least we know it's had something to eat!'

'Yeah, crisps,' James said. 'But that's not much for a hungry dog, is it?'

'No,' Mandy agreed. Maybe they should start putting food down themselves, which would make it easier to get near the timid little dog.

'Hi!' Charlie said, looking up to greet Mandy and James the moment they walked into the grotto room. He was sprawled on the floor in his tartan dressing-gown and bright yellow pyjamas. Sheets of paper were spread out on the floor all round him. He was sticking glitter in the outlines of bold letters drawn on them. 'It's going to be a banner. For the front of the grotto!' Charlie explained, flashing them a wide grin.

Grandad winked. 'It was your Gran's idea,' he whispered to Mandy and James. 'Charlie's spent all morning getting the lettering just right. He hasn't said he's bored once!'

'Good idea, Gran!' Mandy grinned. She told her grandparents about seeing the Jack Russell again. 'Did you notice a little brown-and-white dog in the car park when you arrived?'

Gran shook her head. 'No, dear. We didn't see any dogs, did we, Tom?'

Grandad shook his head.

Charlie jumped up. 'Is the dog outside again? Let's go and see it!'

'No. It's gone now,' Mandy explained. 'It came over to me, but the guard startled it and it ran off again. We don't know where it is now.'

'Oh,' Charlie grumbled. 'I really wanted to stroke it.'

'The guard said it pinched a little girl's crisps,' James told him.

Charlie laughed, forgetting his disappointment. 'Did it?'

'Oh dear. It could scare people jumping up at them like that.' Gran looked worried. 'It didn't bite her, did it?'

Mandy quickly explained that the little girl had dropped her crisps on the ground in the car park. 'It's a really sweet little dog, Gran. I managed to stroke it before it ran off again.'

'Maybe you'll see it again, as we're going to be here until Christmas Eve. But don't get any ideas about taking home a stray dog,' Gran warned.

'No chance.' Mandy sighed. 'Not with Mum and Dad's rules.'

For the next hour or so, she and James were kept busy. They decorated the collection box for the donated presents. Then they began setting out the raffle prizes on a table.

'This table looks a bit dull,' James said, carefully

balancing a large box of chocolates on its side.

'We could wind tinsel round its legs,' Mandy suggested. 'We've got tons of the stuff!'

'Good idea. I'll get some,' James said.

'Mandy, where are the scissors?' Charlie's cheerful voice interrupted him.

When Mandy had passed him the scissors, Charlie decided he needed some tinsel to decorate the edges of his banner. Mandy was just helping him to fix on the tinsel with sticky tape, when a woman poked her head into the room. She was wearing jeans and a thick jumper. Her fair hair, round face, and blue eyes were similar to Charlie's. She came straight over to them. 'Hi! The nurse said you'd be in here. You two look very busy.'

'Mum!' Charlie jumped up and gave her a hug. 'Look what we're making!' He pointed to the banner.

'That's lovely,' said the woman, ruffling Charlie's hair. She turned to Mandy. 'Thanks for letting Charlie help. I know he can be a handful. He's got energy to spare.'

'He's all right,' Mandy said, smiling. She introduced herself and James. 'And this is my gran and grandad. We're decorating Santa's grotto this year.'

'I'm Linda Kingston,' Charlie's mum said with a friendly smile. She took a box out of her shoulder bag and gave it to Charlie. 'I thought you could use these.' She beamed at Mandy and James. 'My son's quite an artist.'

'Coloured pencils! And a new sketch pad! Thanks, Mum. These are great.'

'What sort of things do you like to draw?' James asked.

Mrs Kingston looked surprised. 'Haven't you shown your new friends your pictures?' she asked her son.

Charlie looked down and shook his head, looking a bit embarrassed. He dug at the floor with the toe of his slipper.

'We'd love to see your pictures, wouldn't we, James?' Mandy said.

James nodded.

'Really?' Charlie's face lit up. 'Come on then. I'll show you. You come too, Mum!'

They all trooped through to the children's ward. There was a huge Christmas tree in one corner and decorations hung from the ceiling.

Charlie led them to his bed. Colourful drawings of animals were pinned up on the wall round it – lions, tigers, and elephants, but pictures of dogs outnumbered them all.

Mandy's eyes widened. 'These are really good.'

'Yeah!' James agreed. ' 'Specially the ones of dogs.'

Linda Kingston smiled proudly. 'Drawing, painting and dogs, that's all my Charlie's interested in. Dog mad, he is. He's got a real way with them too.'

Charlie's blond eyebrows shot together in a fierce frown. 'Shame that you won't allow me to have one then, isn't it!' he burst out, stalking away.

Mandy watched Charlie stomping off down the

ward in the direction of the toilets. His shoulders were hunched and he had thrust his hands into his dressing-gown pockets.

'Oh, dear.' Charlie's mum sank on to the bed. 'I shouldn't have said that.'

'Would you like me to go after him?' James offered.

'Thanks, but it's probably best to let him calm down by himself,' Linda Kingston said with a sigh.

'Why isn't Charlie allowed to have a dog?' Mandy asked curiously. 'Don't you like them?'

'It's not that,' Mrs Kingston said. 'I'd like a dog too. But Charlie and I live in a flat and we don't have a garden for a dog to run around in. Besides, I have to work full-time and you can't leave a dog on its own all day. It wouldn't be fair.'

'No,' Mandy agreed. She glanced at all the drawings of the dogs again. No wonder Charlie had been so interested in the cheeky little Jack Russell in the car park. He was probably hoping it was a stray that needed a home. *His* home!

'I'll wait here for Charlie, if you want to get back to your grandparents,' Mrs Kingston said. 'He'll soon cool off and then he'll probably join you.'

'OK. Tell him we'll see him later.' Mandy and

James retraced their steps back through the children's ward.

'Those dog paintings were fantastic, weren't they?' said James.

'They were brilliant,' Mandy agreed. 'It's a shame Charlie can't have a real dog, though.'

James nodded. 'I couldn't imagine life without Blackie!'

'But you wouldn't have him if you lived in a flat with no garden, would you?'

'No way!' James admitted.

'I hate to say it, but you have to agree with Charlie's mum,' Mandy said. But even though she couldn't argue with Mrs Kingston's sensible attitude, she couldn't help feeling sorry for Charlie.

Four

'Just one last drawing pin. Da-dah!'

Mandy and James were standing on hospital chairs as they finished pinning Charlie's banner above the door to the finished grotto.

Three nurses and some patients from the children's ward had come along for a look. They clapped and cheered as James and Mandy climbed down from their chairs. James reddened, but performed a mock bow, which made everyone laugh.

'The grotto's rather splendid, even if I say so myself!' Gran said.

'Top notch,' Grandad agreed.

And it was. Silver display boards formed three sides of the ice-cave. Two tall rectangular pillars framed the entrance, while small Christmas trees placed on either side of the door added a festive touch. Decorations glittered everywhere, and Charlie's banner wished everyone 'Happy Christmas'.

'Good idea of yours to cover those cardboard boxes to make pillars,' Mandy said to James.

Grandad chuckled. 'And who would have thought that we would use up that entire mountain of tinsel!' He looked at the raffle table, which Mandy and James had decorated. 'Hmm. Hairy tinsel legs. Interesting!'

Mandy laughed. 'We think it looks brilliant, don't we, James?'

James nodded.

'Time for a break,' Gran announced when the nurses and children had gone back to the ward. 'I packed some lunch. Egg and cress sandwiches and home-made flapjack, anyone?'

'Great!' Mandy loved her Gran's cooking, especially her sticky flapjacks.

Gran was just gathering up the paper plates and napkins from their indoor picnic, when the door opened and two young children and their mother looked in.

'We have our first visitors,' announced Grandad, ushering them in.

'We brought some toys for the Christmas appeal,' the woman explained, while the children gazed round-eyed at the ice cave.

'How lovely! Thanks very much,' Gran said. 'The collection bin is over there.'

'And don't forget to buy some raffle tickets!' Mandy reminded them. 'It's in a good cause.'

'And we've got some great prizes,' James put in.

All afternoon there was a steady stream of visits from local children and their parents. The appeal on the radio seemed to be doing the trick.

'Cripes.' James peered into the collection bin which was filling up rapidly. 'At this rate, we're going to need another bin.'

'Good. That means all the children in hospital over Christmas will get lots of presents,' Mandy said. Meanwhile, she took the opportunity to ask everyone she could about the Jack Russell. 'Did you see a little brown-and-white dog on your way into the hospital?'

'No, sorry,' came the reply from three children and their dad. It was the same story from the following two family groups. Then Mandy had some luck.

'Oh, yes! We just saw it!' said a little girl in a red hat.

Mandy's heart leaped. 'Where?'

'Just going into the bushes at the side of the car park,' her mum said. 'Is it your dog?'

The bushes. Mandy's hopes rose. That was where she had seen it the first time. So the little dog was still about. Mandy shook her head. 'We don't know who it belongs to. We think it's a stray.'

'What a shame,' the woman replied. 'It looked a sweet little thing.'

It is, Mandy thought. She felt more and more worried about the Jack Russell. Snow was forecast for the next few days. She hated to think of the dog spending another night outside. There had to be something they could do. She couldn't get the thought of the Jack Russell's appealing face out of her mind.

'I'm going along to visit Percy,' Gran informed Mandy later, when the number of visitors bringing toys and raffle prizes had slowed down a bit. 'Do you want to come with me?'

Mandy jumped up at once and followed her gran along the corridor to Ward Twelve.

'Oh, look!' Mandy saw that Percy was sitting up in bed. The old man was wearing glasses and reading a newspaper. 'He must be feeling stronger.'

'He's certainly a better colour,' Gran agreed, as they approached the bed. 'Hello, Percy. You're looking much better today,' she said brightly.

Percy looked up and peered at them over the top of his glasses. He didn't smile. 'Oh, it's you, Dorothy. Thanks for coming,' he said politely.

'And I've brought my granddaughter, Mandy, to say hello,' Gran said.

'Hi, Mr Green,' Mandy said, smiling.

'Nice of you to come,' Percy murmured. But he kept staring down at the newspaper which lay on the bed, as if he was thinking about something else.

'Mandy's helping us with the grotto.' Gran tried to engage Percy in conversation. 'Her friend James is here too, and Tom, my husband.'

'And there's a boy called Charlie helping us. He's recovering from bronchitis,' Mandy added.

'That's right.' Gran smiled kindly at the old man. 'Perhaps you might like to come and see us all in the grotto later? It's just a short walk down the corridor, past the children's ward.'

'I'm sure the grotto's very nice.' Percy seemed to find talking an effort. 'Thanks for coming to see me, Dorothy. But I'm rather tired. Would you mind . . .' He took off his glasses and lay back against his pillow.

Mandy glanced over at her gran. Percy had closed his eyes and obviously didn't want to chat.

'Well – we'll leave you to rest then,' Gran said. 'We'll call by again, when you feel up to having a visit.'

'Goodbye, Mr Green,' Mandy said quietly. She got no reply. It looked as if Percy might have fallen asleep.

'Oh, dear.' Gran looked worried as she and Mandy walked back to the grotto. 'Percy seems so depressed, not at all like himself. He usually loves to have a chat. I think I'll have a word with Sister Lacey.'

They found the ward sister in her office at the end of the ward. 'Ah, yes,' said Sister Lacey in answer to Gran's enquiry. 'Mr Green. Physically he's almost back to normal. But he does seem very down. I can't quite understand what he's saying. Something about – a twinkle?'

'Twinkle?' Mandy said. 'What on earth does he mean?'

'I think I can help you there,' said a voice from behind them. 'Twinkle is Dad's Jack Russell. I bought him to keep my father company while we were in America. I hope he's all right – I don't know what happened to him when Dad was brought into hospital.'

Mandy, Gran and Sister Lacey turned round. A tall man with dark hair and wearing a smart blue suit stood there. He had a friendly face, but Mandy thought he looked tired.

'Hello, I'm Michael Green. Percy's son,' he introduced himself. 'I've driven straight here from the airport.'

'I'm Dorothy Hope,' Gran said. 'I live in Welford, near Percy. And this is Mandy.'

'Hello, Mr Green,' Mandy said.

'It's very kind of you to visit my father.' Percy's son smiled at Gran and Mandy. 'Please, call me, Michael.'

Mandy smiled back. She liked Percy's son at once.

'Your father will be very pleased to see you,' Sister Lacey said to Michael. 'He's much better. We've got the asthma under control now.'

'Thank goodness for that. I was so worried,' Michael said, then he grinned. 'But by the sound of things, it's Twinkle he wants to see! Dad's always loved Jack Russells. He used to breed them in the old days.'

'Did he?' Mandy was immediately interested.

'I had no idea,' Gran said. 'I used to see Percy when I took his meals on wheels. But I didn't know that he had a dog. Percy never invited me into the house and I got the feeling he liked to keep to himself.'

'That's Dad all right,' Michael said. 'He's a proud man and likes to think that he can manage by himself. That's why I got him Twinkle. Dad might be a bit shy with people, but I knew he wouldn't object to a dog keeping him company!'

Mandy smiled. 'Dogs make wonderful friends, don't they?' she said. A picture of Charlie, who wanted a dog so badly, flashed into her mind.

Michael nodded. 'Dad's still quite a name in terrier racing, you know. He's bred some famous dogs.'

'Really?' Mandy was fascinated by the idea that Percy had bred champion racers. Just wait until she told James – and Charlie!

'Oh, yes. Get him talking about terrier racing and you can't get a word in edgeways.' Michael turned to the ward sister. 'I think I'll go and see him now. If I can tell him about Twinkle, he's sure to feel much better.'

Sister Lacey nodded and smiled. Then she picked up a clipboard from the desk and bustled back out to her wards.

Michael turned back to Mandy and her gran. 'By the way, who is looking after Twinkle while Dad's in hospital?'

There was an awkward silence. Michael looked from Gran to Mandy. 'Is Twinkle with Dad's next-door neighbour?' he prompted.

'I'm not sure.' Gran looked rather worried. 'I don't think anyone realised that Percy had a pet dog. As I said, *I* certainly didn't. Not until you just told me.'

'What?' Michael frowned. 'But Twinkle must have been with dad when he was brought into hospital. Didn't someone see him?'

'Oh.' Mandy suddenly put two and two together. 'I think I might have seen Twinkle,' she burst out.

'Did you? Where?' Michael asked.

'In the car park,' Mandy told him. 'I've seen him a couple of times. A porter and a guard said that a Jack Russell has been hanging around outside the hospital for a couple of days. And some of the kids visiting the grotto today saw him as well. It's got to be Twinkle—'

'Slow down a minute, Mandy love,' Gran interrupted. 'It could be coincidence. Walton's quite a way from Welford. How would Twinkle have got here?'

Mandy frowned. Gran had a point. But she was sure that the stray was Twinkle.

'Didn't you say that you managed to get close to the dog this morning?' Gran said.

'Yes, that's right,' Mandy answered.

'So you got a good look at him? Can you describe him?' Michael asked.

'He's almost all white,' Mandy said, 'with brown ears and a patch of brown over one eye. I managed to stroke him, but he ran off. Then James and I spoke to the guard and he told us about Twinkle pinching some crisps.'

Michael ran a hand through his dark hair. He looked worried. 'It certainly sounds like our Twinkle. Especially the crisps! He's a bit of a rascal. Can you show me where you last saw him? I ought to see if I can catch him.'

'I'll help you,' Mandy said. 'If we go by the grotto, we can pick up James. He'll want to look for Twinkle too.'

'Those two are always on hand in any animal

emergency,' Gran said to Michael with a smile. 'Animal mad, both of them.'

Michael glanced down at Mandy. 'Well, if you and James can lead me to Twinkle, you'll be doing me a huge favour. I'm really worried about him being loose on the streets. And I dread to think how Dad's going to react if his best friend's gone missing.'

'Oh, dear,' Gran said. 'That could really set poor Percy back.'

'But when we find him, Percy will be delighted, won't he?' Mandy pointed out.

'My granddaughter's such an optimist,' Gran said. 'I'll help you look as well. Tom won't mind keeping an eye on the grotto.'

'Right, I'll meet you all in the car park in a few minutes,' Michael said, beginning to walk away. 'I'm going to pop along and see how Dad is doing first. But I don't know what I'm going to say if he asks me about Twinkle . . .'

Mandy hurried back along the corridor to fetch James. They just had to find Twinkle, for Percy's sake.

But finding him was one thing; catching him would be another.

* * *

'What?' Mandy looked blankly at James. She had just finished telling him about Twinkle.

James was holding up his hands and waving them about. He shook his head and mouthed silently, No. No.

Suddenly, an eager voice rang out. 'I'm coming to help look for Twinkle too!'

'Uh-oh.' Mandy pulled a face. She hadn't realised that Charlie had appeared in the doorway behind her.

'I was trying to tell you that he was listening,' James hissed.

'Now, Charlie,' Grandad took charge, 'you know you have to stay inside the hospital. You can help me here in the grotto.'

Charlie's face fell. 'I'm fed up of being in here,' he grumbled. 'I can't do anything.'

'I know, lad,' Grandad sympathised. 'It's not much fun being sick is it? But I'm sure Mandy and James will tell you if they find Twinkle, won't you?'

'Course we will,' Mandy agreed warmly.

'Can I help you look after Twinkle when you find him?' Charlie asked Mandy.

'Hang on,' said Grandad. 'We don't know that it definitely *is* Twinkle yet.'

'I do!' Charlie said, a look of certainty on his face. 'I can't wait to see him. He sounds great.'

Mandy smiled. She felt just the same!

Just then, Gran popped her head round the door. 'Are you ready, you two?' she asked. Mandy and James grabbed their jackets and followed Gran out to the car park. They stopped outside the door and looked around. There were lots of cars and people about – but no little brown-and-white dog.

'Here's Michael now,' Gran said. 'How's Percy feeling?' she asked as Michael came up to them.

'He was pleased to see me.' Michael smiled. He was looking much more relaxed now. 'Couldn't believe it was me at first. He thought I was still in the States.'

'Did he ask about Twinkle?' Mandy asked.

Michael nodded. 'I said I wasn't sure who was looking after him, which isn't exactly a lie, but I promised that I would go and find out. Is there any sign of Twinkle yet?'

'No,' Gran answered, shaking her head.

'Oh, dear. I hope nothing's happened to him,' Michael said. 'Car parks can be dangerous places for loose dogs.'

'Maybe he's staying out of sight while it's so busy?' James suggested.

'Yes,' Mandy said. 'Twinkle's had one near miss already, with an ambulance. I don't think he'd go near any of the cars.'

James nodded in agreement. 'There's lots of places around here for him to hide.' He waved his arm towards the thick bushes which ran along either side of the car park. Beyond the shrubs, the hospital lawns stretched away to thick woodland on one side, and a housing estate on the other. If Twinkle had decided to venture out of the hospital grounds, it might be impossible to find him.

'Right. Where shall we start looking?' Gran went into action mode.

'Shall you and I work our way up and down the rows of parked cars?' Michael suggested to Gran.

'And James and I could start looking over by those bushes,' Mandy said. 'Twinkle's been seen there a few times.' She looked at James, who nodded, and they headed off across the tarmac.

'Maybe Twinkle's made himself a den.' James's logical mind ran on ahead. 'He might have found somewhere sheltered to sleep.'

'Good thinking,' Mandy said. 'I'll check behind all the bushes and trees in these borders.'

'And I'll check those sheds over there,' said

James, pointing to a group of wooden outbuildings which stood at the edge of the lawn, on the woodland side of the grounds.

Mandy spent a few minutes searching under bushes, then made her way round to the area where the waste bins were kept. Even though she hadn't spotted the Jack Russell there before, it was the sort of place where a dog might go to look for food.

'Mandy! Over here.' It was James's voice. Mandy hurried around the corner of the hospital towards the sound.

James was standing next to the wall. 'Look at this!' he said.

Mandy saw that a huge silvery pipe led down from the hospital's upper floors. The base of it entered the wall about half a metre above the ground.

'What is it? It looks like a heating duct or something,' she said. She could feel hot air wafting round her knees, where the pipe joined the wall.

'It is!' James said. 'And look at this.' He bent down and pulled an old cardboard box from underneath the bottom of the pipe. There was a crumpled crisp wrapper in the corner of the box and a few white hairs on the bottom of the box, as if a hairy white body had been lying there recently. 'I reckon Twinkle's been sleeping in here.'

'Oh, yes!' Mandy admired the little dog's cleverness. 'What a great hidy-hole!'

James looked around him, frowning. 'So – where is he now?'

Mandy shrugged. 'He could be anywhere. I guess we keep on looking.'

Suddenly there was a yell. 'Oi! Come back with those, you cheeky little tyke!'

Mandy and James looked at each other. 'Isn't that . . .' Mandy began.

'Yes!' said James, quickly. It was the voice of the security guard they had spoken to yesterday.

'Come on!' Mandy took off across the tarmac. She rounded a corner, with James hard on her heels. Racing across the car park, away from the guard's security cabin, was a small brown-and-white dog.

'Twinkle!' Mandy called out.

At the sound of his name, the dog turned. He gave a short bark and stood still.

'Is that his name?' the guard said. He went over to a rather squashed, plastic-wrapped package, which lay on the ground, and picked it up. 'The little perisher was just about to pinch my sandwiches,' he grumbled. 'I only turned my back for a minute and he nipped in through the door and whipped them off the table! They're cheese and pickle too. My favourite!'

Mandy's lips twitched. She saw that James was trying not to laugh. Then she grew serious. Twinkle was still standing just a few metres away. 'This is the best chance we have of catching him,' she whispered to James.

James nodded. 'Let's try and get a bit closer to him.'

Mandy and James moved forward slowly.

Twinkle watched them closely. Every time they moved, he backed away. The little dog whined, his tail hanging between his legs. Mandy's heart sank. He seemed so wary. His brown ears were flat and his muscles were tense.

'I think he wants to come to us, but he's worried that he's going to get in trouble for pinching those sandwiches,' James reasoned.

'You could be right.' Mandy saw that Twinkle was darting backwards and forwards on his tiny paws, looking uncertain whether to take off again. 'Poor little thing. He must be so cold and hungry,' she said. Just then, a car door slammed. Twinkle froze, his ears straining towards the sound, and then he raced off behind the security cabin and disappeared into the bushes again. Mandy thought of Percy lying in his bed, worrying about Twinkle. He was going to be so upset when he knew that his dog was running around loose. They needed something to coax Twinkle into coming closer. But what?

'James!' she burst out suddenly. 'I've just had a brilliant idea!'

Five

James listened carefully while Mandy outlined her plan.

'Great idea!' he said. 'I'll go and fetch it right now. It's still in my holdall.' He zoomed away and disappeared through the main entrance of the hospital.

'Fetch what?' Gran had just arrived at the security cabin with Michael beside her. 'I know that look, Mandy Hope. What are you and James plotting?'

'We need something to persuade Twinkle to come nearer, right?' Mandy began.

'Right,' Gran agreed. 'What are you going to use?'

'Well – Twinkle must be starving hungry,' Mandy said. 'He's just tried to sneak off with the guard's sandwiches—'

'Is he here, then?' Michael looked around hopefully.

Mandy shook her head. 'He was, but he ran away just now when someone made a noise. I don't think he went far, though. James and I thought we could use some kind of food to tempt Twinkle nearer when he comes back.'

'Good thinking, Mandy.' Michael smiled at her. 'Tell you what, why don't I give Twinkle a call to see if he appears?'

'OK,' said Mandy. 'He might recognise your voice. Try over there first.' She pointed to the bushes behind the security cabin.

Michael walked over and put his hands up to his mouth. 'Twinkle!' he called. 'Twinkle! Come here, boy!'

There was a rustle under one of the bushes, and a white nose peeped out. Mandy crouched down and peered into the leaves. Two big brown eyes blinked nervously in the gloom. Mandy held out her hand. 'It's all right, boy,' she said in a soft calm voice. 'No one's going to hurt you.'

Twinkle took a cautious step forward. Mandy

didn't move a muscle. Twinkle gave a little whine and walked out further. He looked around him, still tense and ready to run away.

'Well done, Mandy,' Michael said quietly.

Just then James burst out of the hospital doors and came running back across to them. He arrived red-faced and out of breath. 'Oh, good. Twinkle's here!' James gasped. He came to a halt a few metres away. Twinkle watched him, but he didn't run away. James unzipped his coat and pulled out a long object covered in red-and-green cellophane. He held it up. It was Blackie's Christmas stocking.

'Right. Thanks, James.' Mandy didn't waste any time. She stood up and went over to James. Ripping open the cellophane, she took out a bag of doggy treats. She glanced across to the narrow strip of lawn beside the bushes where Twinkle was now standing. His ears were down and he kept licking his lips nervously. *Just hang on a bit longer, Twinkle*, Mandy pleaded silently.

'Where did that stocking come from?' Michael said to James.

'I bought it this morning at the pet shop. Think of it as a present to Twinkle – from my dog, Blackie!' James replied, with a grin.

Gran turned to Mandy. 'I wonder whether Michael should try and catch Twinkle. He did come back when Michael called him, didn't he?'

Michael shook his head. 'Actually, Twinkle's not that used to me at all. He spent all his time with Dad, and I've been out of the country for months. I think you should try, Mandy. Twinkle came to you earlier. And he listened to you again just now.'

'OK.' Mandy didn't waste time arguing. She moved forward slowly. She hoped Twinkle would remember her. He had let her scratch his chest and stroke his ears earlier that morning. Maybe he would trust her enough to take some of the dog treats. 'Here, boy,' she called. She put a few biscuits on the palm of her hand and held them out temptingly. 'Come and see what I've got for you.'

At first Twinkle backed away. Then he lifted his nose and took a long, deep sniff. His ears shot upright and he began to wag his tail.

He can smell the treats, Mandy thought. She took a few more steps nearer to him. 'That's it. Come on. These are for you.' She rustled the bag encouragingly. Twinkle's ears twitched at the tempting sound. Mandy's whole body was tense. Would her plan work?

Just then a car pulled up behind her, looking for a parking space. Twinkle shied away and darted sideways, peering over his shoulder nervously.

'Oh, no!' Mandy remembered the ambulance. She was afraid that Twinkle would take off again, even though he was hungry. Then they would have to start all over again.

'Now what do we do?' Michael sounded as if he was out of ideas.

Suddenly Mandy remembered one of Blackie's dog training classes. 'When you call a dog towards you, you have to be really enthusiastic,' the instructor had said. 'The dog has to think he's missing out on something wonderful.'

Mandy poured a few more treats into her hand. 'Mmm. These taste lovely!' she said, in a high-pitched, excited voice. She pretended to be eating them, smacking her lips. 'Yummy!' Out of the corner of her eye, she watched Twinkle, who was crouched under one of the bushes.

Twinkle put his head on one side. He seemed to be listening to Mandy as she tucked into his biscuits. Then he gave a little yelp of excitement and trotted towards her.

Mandy beamed as Twinkle pushed his cold nose

into her hand. 'Oh, good boy!' she praised him.

Twinkle crunched up all the dog treats. Then he gave a sharp bark. More please, he seemed to be saying.

'You must be starving, you poor boy!' Mandy fed Twinkle more of the treats as James, Michael, and Gran walked cautiously towards them.

'You ought to be an actress,' Michael said. 'You nearly had me trotting over to sample those dog treats!'

Twinkle didn't look up as the others approached. He just kept eating, his long tail wagging frantically.

'Look at that! He's almost scoffed the whole stocking,' James said, crouching down and stroking Twinkle's ears. 'I'll have to go and get another one for Blackie.'

'Oh, sorry, James.' Mandy felt a bit guilty. 'I hadn't realised how hungry Twinkle was!'

'It doesn't matter. I'm glad we were able to catch him,' James said.

Suddenly Twinkle stopped eating. Mandy slowly stretched out her fingers and took hold of his collar, in case he decided to run away again. But the little dog didn't seem to want to go anywhere. He gave a friendly whine, then reached up and began licking James's chin.

'He's saying "Thanks for the treats," ' Mandy said, laughing.

'I think you're right!' Michael patted James on the shoulder. 'That was a great idea!'

'Maybe someone should go and tell Percy that Twinkle's all right?' Mandy suggested.

'You read my mind,' Michael said. 'He'll be so pleased to know that Twinkle is OK.'

'I told you they were expert animal rescuers!' Gran patted her hair, where a few grey strands had escaped from her bun.

'Mandy, could you bring Twinkle over to my car?' Michael asked. 'I don't want him running off again while I go and see Dad.'

Mandy carefully picked up the little dog and held him in her arms. Twinkle gave a contented yap and his mouth lolled open in a doggy grin.

Gran laughed. 'Wouldn't it be lovely if Percy could actually see that Twinkle's all right?' she said, reaching out and smoothing Twinkle's white coat. The dog was surprisingly clean, considering he had been living rough for a couple of days.

Michael nodded. 'But he's going to have to wait until he gets home for that.'

'Maybe not!' Mandy said. Gran had given her an idea.

'What do you mean?' James asked.

'Well – Ward Twelve is on the ground floor, isn't it?' Mandy answered, warming to her idea. 'And Percy's bed is next to a window. If someone holds Twinkle up, Percy could see him.'

'That's a great idea!' said James. He began working out Percy's exact whereabouts. 'The children's ward is in that wing.' He pointed across the car park. 'So the grotto room must be there. Then Ward Twelve is just round the corner over there.'

Still holding Twinkle, Mandy led the way past the hospital entrance and round the corner. A long paved area ran along the length of the wing, underneath the windows. Comfortable-looking wooden benches stood along the wall, where patients could sit and enjoy the sunshine in warmer weather.

Michael grinned. 'I'll go over there and hold Twinkle up to the window right now. Dad's going to be delighted to see him safe and sound!' He lifted Twinkle out of Mandy's arms. Twinkle tensed briefly, but then relaxed as Mandy slipped him another treat.

'We'll go and tell your Dad to look out of the window,' Mandy volunteered.

'Good idea,' said Michael. 'I'll be waiting.'

'What still puzzles me,' Gran said, as she, Mandy and James made their way through the hospital to Ward Twelve, 'is how Twinkle managed to follow Percy all the way to the hospital.'

'It's a mystery, isn't it?' Mandy said.

'Maybe Percy knows something about it,' James suggested.

They found Percy sitting up in bed, propped against his pillows. He was listening to the radio and looking rather glum.

'Hello again.' Gran gave Percy a huge smile. 'We've brought you some wonderful news.'

'Oh, aye,' Percy said dully. He looked up at them briefly, then down at the bedcovers again.

'It's about Twinkle,' James announced.

'Eh?' Percy sat up straighter. His whole face brightened. 'Twinkle! You've seen him?'

'Oh, yes,' Mandy said. 'He's lovely!'

'And Michael's going to hold ... ow!' James grimaced as Mandy trod on his foot.

'Don't give it away!' she hissed out of the corner of her mouth.

'Sorry.' James hopped about on one foot.

Percy didn't notice. He was craning his neck to peer down the corridor behind them. 'Where's Michael? Has he found out who's looking after Twinkle?'

'He certainly has.' Gran pointed out the window. 'Take a look.'

Mandy saw Michael's face appear at the ground floor window. He waved at his dad. Then he lifted Twinkle up so that the little dog could see into the ward.

Percy's eyes opened wide. He looked amazed. 'Twinkle!' You're here. I can't believe it!'

Twinkle had seen Percy too. He let out a series of high-pitched yaps and wriggled in Michael's arms. His brown ears flapped wildly as he tried to get to his owner.

A huge grin spread across the old man's face. He waved back. 'Well, I never. Well, I never. My little Twinkle's come to see me.'

Michael signalled that he was going to come in and see his dad. He lowered Twinkle again and disappeared out of sight.

Percy sank back against his pillows, a contented smile on his face. 'Oh, it's good to see that little rascal again,' he murmured happily.

'We've been wondering how Twinkle got here.

He's been staying around the hospital grounds for the past few days,' Gran said.

'Is that where he was?' Percy shook his head slowly. 'I should have known that he'd follow me here.'

'But how did he get here?' Mandy asked. 'What happened to Twinkle when you were taken ill?'

Percy looked thoughtful. He took a sip of water and made himself more comfortable on his pillows. 'Well, lass. Twinkle's a bit of an escapologist and I'd got a bit of loose fence in my garden. I didn't want him getting out and running off, did I, so I was in the garden checking out that fence. Then my asthma came on, and I don't really know what happened after that . . .' He trailed off, looking worried.

Mandy's gran reached over and patted his hand. 'Don't worry, Percy,' she said. 'Your neighbour saw you fall over, and they called the ambulance.'

Percy nodded. 'That's right. That's what the sister told me.'

'Was Twinkle with you in the garden?' Mandy asked. She still couldn't work out how Twinkle had known where his owner had gone.

'Yes, he was playing with a ball down at the bottom,' Percy said.

'So Twinkle must have got out of the garden and followed the ambulance?' James guessed. 'Maybe through the hole in the fence?'

'But however did he keep up with the ambulance?' Gran asked.

Mandy wondered about that too. Jack Russells were strong little dogs, but Walton was twenty minutes by car from Welford.

Percy's face creased in a grin. 'I reckon he must have followed the ambulance all the way here. Probably took a few short cuts across the moors to keep up.'

'Wow!' James and Mandy looked at each other in astonishment. Mandy realised that Twinkle must be extremely devoted to his owner.

'Twinkle's as smart as they come,' Percy said. He looked very proud of his enterprising pet. His pale blue eyes were shining and there was a bit of colour in his thin cheeks. 'He'd have been a brilliant racer,' Percy went on. 'Racers have to be smart as well as fast to be winners, you know.'

'Just wait until we tell Charlie all this!' Mandy said to James.

'Charlie? Is that the lad you mentioned earlier?' Percy said. 'The one who's had chest problems like me?'

'That's right. He's had bronchitis,' Mandy told him.

'He's rather bored now that he's feeling better, and he's been helping out at the grotto, hasn't he, Mandy?' James added.

Mandy nodded. 'And Charlie's dog mad. He wanted to come and help look for Twinkle, but he's not allowed outside the hospital yet.'

'Bored is he, eh?' Percy looked amused. 'You tell him to come and see me. If he's keen on dogs, he might like to hear about my terrier racing days.'

'I'm sure he'd love that!' said Mandy. She exchanged a grin with James.

Just then, Michael came striding into the ward. His dark blue suit was speckled with white dog hairs, but he didn't seem to mind. 'Hello again, Dad!' He came straight over and gave Percy a hug. 'It's good to see you looking more cheerful.'

Percy patted his son's back. 'I'm feeling much better, lad. Especially now I know Twinkle's OK! Where have you left him?'

Michael pulled up a chair next to Mandy's gran and sat down. 'In the car I hired at the airport. He'll be fine for an hour or so. I've made a snug bed for him out of a travel rug and left a window open a tiny bit.'

'Inside your car?' Percy looked a bit concerned.

Michael chuckled. 'I know Twinkle's clever but even he can't get out of a locked car! Don't worry. He'll stay put this time.'

'It's not that,' Percy said. 'If Twinkle tries to escape he could do some damage to the seats and what not. He's only small but he's got sharp claws!'

'Oh, I see.' Michael looked none too pleased at the thought of shredded seat covers in his rented car. 'I can't think where else he'd be safe for an hour or so. I guess I'll just have to hope he behaves himself.'

Mandy had an idea. 'I've thought of somewhere. Hang on. I'll be back!' She turned to James. 'Come on!' she said, jumping out of her chair and heading down the ward.

James hurried after her. 'Where are we going?'

Mandy glanced back over her shoulder. 'To have a word with Sister Lacey!'

Six

'And if Twinkle is allowed into the grotto, Percy will feel better because he knows that his dog isn't cooped up in a car. And the people who come to bring presents would enjoy seeing Twinkle.' Mandy stood in the ward sister's office and explained her brilliant idea.

'Hmm. We really couldn't have a dog running about near the wards . . .' Sister Lacey looked doubtful.

'Oh, he wouldn't run around,' Mandy assured her quickly. 'Twinkle's really well behaved. We'd make sure we kept a close eye on him, wouldn't we, James?'

James nodded. Just then, the phone rang. The ward sister smiled at them and answered it. 'Yes? This is Sister Lacey speaking.'

'Twinkle – well-behaved!' James whispered, raising his eyebrows at Mandy. 'Have you forgotten about him stealing those sandwiches?'

'No.' Mandy looked determined. 'But I call that showing initiative! Twinkle will be fine now he's had something to eat, and seen Percy again, of course.'

'I hope so!' James said quietly. He sounded less confident than Mandy.

'OK. Bye.' The ward sister put down the phone and turned back to Mandy and James. 'Sorry about that. All right. I've decided that you can bring Twinkle inside. But you must be responsible for him.'

'Great! Thanks very much!' Mandy said delightedly.

'Let's go and tell Percy and Michael,' James said.

They hurried back to Ward Twelve. Mandy blurted out the good news the minute she reached Percy's bedside. 'We've got permission to bring Twinkle into the hospital – he's going to be allowed into the grotto!'

'Well I never,' Percy said. His blue eyes twinkled

at her. 'How did you manage that?'

'Mandy can be very determined where animals are concerned!' Gran told him, passing the end of his bed with a tray of jugs. She had busied herself filling water jugs and tidying up the vases of flowers while Percy spent some time with his son.

Mandy grinned. 'Well, they can't speak up for themselves, can they?'

'There you are, Dad. You can be sure Twinkle will be in good hands.' Michael seemed delighted by Mandy and James's news too.

'Yes.' Percy looked relaxed and happy now. 'And will young Charlie be there too?' he asked.

Mandy nodded. 'I expect so. Especially if he knows there's a dog around.'

Percy chuckled. 'Don't forget to tell Charlie to come and visit me. I reckon we've got a few things in common.'

Gran looked at Mandy with a slight frown. 'Speaking of Charlie,' she said, 'you ought to go back and rescue your grandad. That boy might have worn him out by now!'

Mandy grinned. 'Don't worry, Gran, I'm sure Grandad's kept him busy. Anyway, he was only worried about Twinkle.'

'Best go along and tell Charlie you found him then,' Percy said to Mandy and James. 'We can't have the lad worrying.'

'I'll stay with Dad, if that all right with you. We have a lot of news to catch up on.' Michael stood up and took the belt off his raincoat. 'Here you are. You can use this as a lead for Twinkle.'

'Good idea. Thanks.' Mandy pocketed the belt. She looked at James. 'Have we got any of those dog treats left?'

James felt in one of his pockets and fished out a crumpled packet of biscuits. 'Yup,' he said, waving them at Mandy. 'Although I can't believe that Twinkle could still be hungry.'

Michael handed them his car keys. 'No need to bring them back. I'll collect them when I pick Twinkle up from the grotto.'

'OK,' Mandy said. She waved goodbye to her gran, who was almost hidden by an enormous bunch of flowers belonging to a man at the end of the ward. Then she and James headed back to the car park.

'Now . . . which is Michael's car?' James scanned the car park.

'Maybe that one?' Mandy said innocently. 'The

one with the Jack Russell looking out of the side window!' She went over to the smart silver car and unlocked the door. Twinkle scrabbled through the seats and greeted her with an enthusiastic lick.

'Come on, boy,' said Mandy as she slipped Michael's belt through his collar. As soon as the makeshift lead was on, Twinkle settled down and hopped obediently out of the car. After locking the car again, Mandy and James walked back across the car park and into the hospital, with Twinkle trotting calmly beside them.

'Cool!' Charlie's eyes nearly popped out of his head as Mandy led Twinkle into the grotto. 'Mr Hope! Look who's here!'

Grandad had been adding more prizes to the display on the table. He came over and gave Mandy a hug. 'So your stray *was* Twinkle after all? Clever old you!' He bent down and ruffled Twinkle's ears. The little dog responded with a friendly lick.

Just then Gran came back into the grotto. 'I've left Percy chatting to his son. He really seems to have perked up in the last hour.' She glanced at the piled-up raffle prizes and overflowing bin of donated presents. 'My word, you've been busy, Tom!'

'Good thing I had some help, wasn't it, lad?' Grandad said to Charlie.

But Charlie didn't answer. He was already on his knees, making friends with Twinkle. 'How come you've brought Twinkle in here? Is he hungry? Can I stroke him?' Charlie's questions tumbled over each other.

As Mandy and James explained how they had finally caught Twinkle, the terrier stood patiently at their feet, looking up at them with his mouth open as if he was smiling. He seemed to know everyone was talking about him.

'He certainly seems like a friendly little dog,' Grandad remarked.

'Course he is!' Charlie said at once. 'Jack Russells are brilliant dogs. Twinkle's just the best!' He held up one finger and said firmly, 'Sit, Twinkle.'

Twinkle promptly sat down. His tail thumped against the floor as he looked up at Charlie expectantly.

'Good boy,' Charlie said. 'It's much nicer in here than in that car park, isn't it?'

Twinkle cocked his head and gave a gruff little bark.

'Look at Twinkle. He's listening to Charlie's

every word,' Mandy whispered to James.

James answered in a low voice. 'I reckon they're two of a kind. Both full of mischief!'

Mandy chuckled. James was right!

'I'm going to ask the nurse for a bowl,' Charlie decided. 'Twinkle wants a drink.' He dashed out into the ward. A couple of minutes later he returned carrying a plastic bowl filled with water. 'There you are.' Charlie put the bowl on the floor.

Twinkle began lapping up the water with his small pink tongue. Charlie watched with a grin on his face. 'Look at that! He was really thirsty.'

'I'm not surprised after all those dog treats!' Gran commented. 'Now it's all very well to make sure that Twinkle is fed and watered, but what about us? I'm famished!'

Mandy glanced at her watch and noticed with surprise that it was long past lunch-time.

Beside her, James nodded his head eagerly. 'I'm starving, too,' he said.

Gran laughed. 'It's a good job I brought us some lunch, then, isn't it? Give me a hand with this, please, James.'

James darted forward and helped Mandy's gran heave a basket on to an empty table. He delved into it and started handing out packets of sandwiches.

They were just finishing their lunch when a new batch of people arrived with more wrapped toys for the Christmas appeal. Gran, Grandad, Mandy and James soon had their hands full seeing to the visitors. James helped to stack the presents in front of the display boards, once the collection bin was full. Mandy was in charge of the raffle table. The tickets were selling like hot cakes.

'Would you like me to look after Twinkle?' Charlie offered eagerly. He had been back up to his ward for some lunch and a check-up, but he soon reappeared, making straight for Twinkle, who was sitting under the raffle table. Mandy had fastened one end of the makeshift lead to a table leg to prevent him from getting away again.

'You'll have to careful that he doesn't run about,' Mandy said. 'We can't have him tripping up the visitors.'

Charlie looked serious. 'OK. I'll just play with Twinkle quietly,' he promised. He untied the belt and began to lead Twinkle round the back of the grotto. 'I know! I'm going to make him something.'

'What are you going to make him?' James asked,

as Charlie squeezed past him.

Charlie lifted his chin. 'It's a secret!' he said importantly, disappearing behind the foil-covered display boards.

'Don't worry,' said Mandy. 'He can't get up to much back there. There's only a few bits of cardboard and some leftover decorations.'

'Mandy! James!' Gran called to them. It was getting hectic again in the grotto and their help was needed.

Fifteen minutes later Charlie came out from behind the screen. He looked very pleased with himself. 'Stay. That's a good boy.' Charlie said to Twinkle, who was still out of sight. 'Everyone, get ready!'

Mandy and James looked round in surprise. Gran, Grandad and the people visiting the grotto all stopped what they were doing. Charlie had everyone's full attention.

Mandy wondered what Charlie had been up to with Twinkle. There hadn't been a sound from either of them, apart from an occasional rustling and a muffled giggle from Charlie.

'Come on out, Twinkle!' Charlie called.

Twinkle trotted into view. Fixed to his head by

bright red ribbons were two small antlers! They were made from cardboard, and rather wobbly, which gave him a lopsided appearance. Twinkle didn't seem to mind wearing them at all. His whole body wriggled and his tail wagged nineteen to the dozen, as he padded into the middle of the room.

Mandy and James burst out laughing. 'With that headgear I reckon he can be Dad's – I mean Santa's – honorary reindeer,' said Mandy.

There was a ripple of applause from the grotto's

visitors. A sturdy toddler dashed forward, arms extended, ready to make a grab for Twinkle.

Mandy tensed. She knew that dogs sometimes found small children unsettling.

She was about to move forward, when Charlie sprang into action. 'Sit, Twinkle,' he said calmly.

Twinkle gave a short bark. Then he sat down with his nose in the air. The toddler threw his arms around Twinkle's neck and squeezed tight. Twinkle didn't blink an eyelid. The friendly little dog seemed to be taking all the fuss in his stride.

'Nice doggie!' The toddler stroked Twinkle's back with a pudgy hand.

'Well done.' Gran patted Charlie's shoulder. 'You handled that well.'

'I'm going to make sure Twinkle behaves himself,' Charlie said seriously. 'Lie down, Twinkle.'

Twinkle promptly sank down. He lay on the floor and put his head between his front paws. His brown-and-white eyebrows moved up and down as he watched Charlie closely.

'Good boy.' Charlie patted Twinkle's head.

'Look at that!' Mandy was very impressed. 'Twinkle's being as good as gold!'

'Charlie's really great with him, isn't he?' James said.

'He's a natural!' Mandy agreed. 'What a shame he can't have a dog of his own.'

An hour later Michael called by to fetch Twinkle. Mandy and James went over to have a word with him.

'How's your dad feeling?' Mandy asked.

'Much better, thanks,' Michael told them. 'In fact, he's so much stronger that Sister Lacey says he'll probably be allowed out of bed tomorrow.'

'That's great news!' Mandy said.

Tomorrow was Sunday, the day before Christmas Eve. It looked as if Percy might be well enough to go home for Christmas.

Twinkle was in the centre of an admiring group of grown-ups and children. He sat with his head in the air, his tail thudding on the floor, as two small children petted him.

'What's Twinkle got on his head?' Michael caught a glimpse of Twinkle as the children moved away. 'Oh, my goodness . . . antlers!' A huge smile spread across Michael's face.

'It was Charlie's idea to make them,' Mandy explained, pointing to Charlie, who was standing on the other side of the grotto, examining one of the presents.

Michael seemed to be trying not to laugh. 'They're very realistic. And Twinkle certainly seems to like them.'

Charlie looked over to them. 'Hi, I'm Charlie,' he said to Michael. 'Twinkle is going to be a pretend reindeer for Santa.'

'Hello, Charlie.' Michael grinned down at the boy. 'That sounds like a great idea.'

Charlie nodded and bent down to straighten one of the antlers, which had flopped forward. 'I don't think Twinkle minds, you know,' he said seriously. 'I wouldn't have made him wear the antlers if he didn't want to.'

'I'd better take Twinkle home with me now,' Michael said. He smiled at Mandy's gran. 'I'm staying at Dad's house over Christmas, so the nurses can get in touch with me if they need to.'

Charlie carefully untied Twinkle's antlers. 'I'll keep these safe for when he wants them again,' he said.

'You do that,' said Michael. 'In fact, Charlie, I was going to ask you a favour.'

'Oh?' Charlie glanced up at the tall man, looking puzzled.

'Yes,' Michael went on, 'if you get time, would you mind popping along to Ward Twelve to visit my dad? He's bound to be missing Twinkle and it might cheer him up if you told him about the antlers.'

Charlie's face brightened. 'OK. No problem! I'd like to meet him.'

Mandy turned to Charlie. 'Oh, I almost forgot to tell you. Percy, Michael's dad, used to breed racing terriers.'

'Did he? Cool!' Charlie said. 'I'd like to breed dogs when I grow up.' He looked down at Twinkle again, and ran his hand along the smooth white coat.

Michael took hold of Twinkle's makeshift lead. 'I've got to go now. I've brought some work back with me and I'd better get started on it. See you all tomorrow.'

'Bye.' James and Charlie waved as Michael went out of the grotto with Twinkle trotting beside him, his claws clicking against the hard floor.

Mandy waved too, but something had begun to bother her.

James took one look at Mandy's face. 'What's wrong?' he asked.

'I was just thinking,' she said worriedly. 'If Michael's got so much work to do – who's going to take Twinkle for walks?'

Seven

Mandy poured herself a bowl of cereal and ate it looking out of the kitchen window, admiring the frosty, bare branches of the trees in the garden. Although it was Sunday morning, there were only two more days before Christmas, and there was lots to do in the surgery. The hospital grotto, however, *was* ready for Santa's visits.

Twinkle was on her mind as she finished her cereal. She wondered if Michael had found time to take him for a morning walk. She rinsed the bowl in the sink and went into the residential unit.

'Hello, love.' Mrs Hope was already there,

studying one of the clipboards which held a patient's notes.

'Have you looked at Peaches yet?' Mandy asked.

'No.' Emily Hope shook her head. 'But I've checked the kitten with the swollen leg, the poodle with the eye infection, and the rat with a stomach tumour. I left Peaches until last. I thought you might like to check on her!'

'Thanks, Mum.' Mandy looked into Peaches' cage.

The guinea-pig was snuffling about in her straw. She gave a throaty little grunt and came over to the bars of the cage.

'How are you today?' Mandy poked her finger inside and tickled Peaches's nose. She could see the bare shaved patch on the guinea pig's side. The wound site looked clean. 'No signs of inflammation,' she reported to her mum. 'Peaches's eyes look bright and her nose is nice and clean.'

Mrs Hope came over to look too. 'She seems quite alert this morning,' she observed.

'She's doing really well!' Mandy was thrilled by Peaches' progress. 'Can I give her a treat?'

Her mum nodded. 'There's lots of fresh vegetables to choose from. But no brassicas, remember.'

'OK.' Mandy knew that guinea-pigs loved celery. She cut a piece, then undid the cage and put it inside. Peaches' pink nose twitched. She came forward and butted the celery. Her little round-tipped tongue poked out and she took a tiny taste.

'Look!' Mandy said excitedly. 'She's interested in it. That's a good sign, isn't it?'

'It certainly is!' Emily Hope nodded. 'I think there's a good chance that Peaches will be going home for Christmas. I know Laura will be pleased. Her mum said she had really missed Peaches when I spoke to her on the phone this morning.'

As Mandy changed the guinea-pig's bedding and checked her water bottle, she began to think about Twinkle again. She wondered if Twinkle still missed Percy. The little dog wouldn't want to stay at home if Michael had no time to give him some attention. 'Got it!' she burst out. 'Got to go, Mum! See you later.'

'Off on a mission?' her mum asked, giving her a shrewd look.

'Yes. Operation Twinkle! And James is going to help. But he doesn't know it yet!' Mandy replied, dashing off to the phone.

James answered on the third ring. 'Hello?'

'Hi, James. Can you meet me at Gran's?' Mandy

came straight to the point. 'I've just had a great idea.'

'Uh-oh! Another one!' James joked, but he sounded interested. 'Fine. I'll be there as soon as I've had breakfast.'

'Great. And bring Blackie with you!' Mandy put down the phone and dashed upstairs to put on a thick jumper and warm boots.

'Hello, Mandy, love. I saw you from the window.' Gran opened the door to Lilac Cottage as Mandy reached the garden path. She looked up at the yellow white sky. 'If you ask me, that sky is full of snow,' she warned.

'I hope so!' Mandy said. 'I love white Christmases. Oh, good. Here's James.'

'Hi, Mandy. Hi, Mrs Hope.' James struggled to stop Blackie jumping up as he opened the gate and walked carefully down the frosty path.

'Hello, Blackie!' Mandy bent down to stroke the Labrador's velvety ears. Blackie pushed his cold wet nose into Mandy's hand. He wriggled vigorously, inviting her to fuss him.

Gran laughed. 'Are you coming in or staying out there for a wrestling match with Blackie?'

'We're going over to Percy's house,' Mandy told her.

'We are?' James looked puzzled. 'What for?'

'To take Twinkle out while Michael works,' Mandy explained.

'Oh, right!' James said. 'Blackie will love that. Do you think we could take Twinkle over to see Percy?'

'I could give you a lift over to Walton later if you like,' Gran offered. 'I've promised to call in on a friend who's going away for Christmas.'

'Thanks, Gran. That would be great,' Mandy said. 'What time shall we come back?'

Gran thought for a moment. 'If you give me an hour, I'll have time to bake some mince-pies too. I'll make enough for you to take some to Percy.'

'OK. See you later.' Then, following Gran's directions, Mandy and James set off for Percy's house, which was not far from Lilac Cottage. Blackie leaped beside them on his lead, jerking James's arm in its socket until James ordered him to calm down.

They had to knock on the door twice before Michael opened it. He came to the door wearing jeans and a sweater. 'Hello again.' He gave them a rather hasty grin and drew his hand through his hair. 'Sorry, I was in the middle of a report.'

'We thought you might be busy,' Mandy said.

'So we wondered if we could take Twinkle out for a walk and then to see Percy. Gran can give us a lift.'

'We've brought Blackie because he's really friendly and loves playing with other dogs,' James added. 'Twinkle would be doing us a favour if he could tire him out!'

'That's very thoughtful of you both. Thank you, that would be great.' Michael patted Blackie's head. 'Hello there, fella! He's a handsome dog, isn't he? Look, I don't mean to be rude, but I really must get on . . .'

'That's OK. Shall I come in and get Twinkle?' Mandy asked.

Michael showed Mandy through to the kitchen, while James waited outside with Blackie. Twinkle was curled up in his bed, warm and snug beside the radiator. As soon as he saw her, he lifted his head and gave a short bark. He leaped up and trotted forward, his tail twirling around madly.

'Hello, boy.' Mandy bent down and gave Twinkle a cuddle, then clipped on his lead, which she found hanging beside the back door.

'See you later,' she called out as she passed the open sitting-room door.

Michael glanced up from his laptop. 'Thanks

very much, Mandy. You and James are real life-savers! I'll tell Dad how helpful you've been when I go to see him later.'

Blackie dashed across the field after Twinkle. Both dogs flew over the frozen ground, their paws making dark tracks in the frosty grass.

'Look at them go!' Mandy said.

Suddenly Twinkle whipped round and came to a full stop. Blackie, being much heavier, shot past and skidded to a clumsy halt. Then Twinkle gave a short bark and lunged forward. Blackie set off after him through the trees.

After a few minutes both dogs trotted back. They were panting heavily, their breath steaming in the crisp air.

Mandy checked her watch. 'We'd better start making our way back to Gran's. She'll be ready to leave by the time we get there. The dogs can have a drink before she gives us a lift to Walton.'

James rubbed his gloved hands together. 'And we can have a mince-pie!' he said appreciatively.

Mandy raised an eyebrow. 'Or two or three, James Hunter!' She knew how much her friend loved Gran's cooking.

At Lilac Cottage the wonderful smell of baking

filled every room. Blackie and Twinkle stretched out on the kitchen floor after their drink, both tired out after the exercise. Mandy and James munched on mince-pies, while Gran packed some of them into a box.

'I've put in a few extra so Percy can offer them around,' she said. 'Help yourself to another one, James.'

'Thanks, Mrs Hope. These are delicious.' James wiped some crumbs from his mouth.

Mandy nudged him gently in the ribs. 'Come on,' she sid. 'If you eat any more, you'll burst. Let's get these dogs in the car before they fall asleep.'

'You two had better sit in the back with the dogs,' Gran suggested. She put the box of mince-pies carefully on the passenger seat, then drove out into the lane.

Blackie and Twinkle behaved perfectly. They hung over the back seat, breathing hot doggy breath on to Mandy and James. At Walton hospital, Gran parked in a space next to the entrance. Mandy and James climbed out and opened the rear door to let the dogs out.

'Can you manage to carry this box?' Gran asked Mandy, eyeing Blackie and Twinkle, who were sniffing eagerly at the tempting baking smells. 'I need to get going now.'

'Oh, yes.' Mandy handed Twinkle's lead to James and took the box. 'Thanks for the lift, Gran. See you later.' Mandy waited while James sorted out the two dogs. 'I'll just take these mince-pies in for Percy,' Mandy said.

'OK. Shall I take the dogs round to the window?' James suggested.

'Good idea,' Mandy replied. 'I'll come straight back and then we can hold Twinkle up for Percy to see.' She made her way to Ward Twelve. Percy was sitting on his bed, wearing a dressing-gown. He was talking to a familiar figure in yellow pyjamas sitting on a chair beside the bed.

'Hello, Percy. Hello, Charlie,' said Mandy.

At the sound of her voice, they both looked up and smiled.

'Charlie's been keeping me company,' Percy explained.

Mandy gave him the box of mince-pies. 'These are a present from Gran,' she said. 'And you've got another visitor outside. Twinkle! He's with James and Blackie. We'll hold him up for you to see in a minute.'

A broad smile spread over Percy's face. 'Oh, that's grand, lass.'

Charlie looked excited. 'Can I see Twinkle too? Mr Green has been telling me all about terrier racing. And we reckon Twinkle would be a champion racer, don't we?'

Percy nodded. 'Charlie can't get enough of my stories. He's wearing me out with all his questions . . .'

But Mandy could tell by his friendly grin that the old man was delighted to have someone to share his memories with. She looked at Charlie, who was leaning back in his chair and peering out of the window, trying to get a glimpse of Twinkle. 'We could bring him into the grotto before we go back to Welford,' Mandy offered.

'Cool!' Charlie said.

Percy smiled at Mandy. 'Good idea,' he said. He turned to Charlie. 'Why don't you go along there and give Twinkle a cuddle from me? Tell him I'll see him soon.'

'OK, I will,' Charlie said delightedly. 'See you there!' He marched off down the ward, munching a mince-pie.

Mandy followed him. As she passed the grotto, she looked in and saw Charlie poking around among the piles of shiny wrapped presents. She smiled to herself.

James was looking a bit flushed. 'I'm glad you're back. These two are a real handful!'

Blackie barked. He jumped up and put his front paws on the hospital wall. His nose was almost level with the windowsill. Twinkle did exactly the same, but his nose was a long way below the window.

'I think they both want to see Percy!' Mandy said. 'Do you think we can manage that?'

'No problem!' James wrapped his arms round Blackie and managed to lift him just high enough to see into the window. Mandy scooped Twinkle up more easily.

Percy's face lit up with amazement when he saw both dogs. He smiled and waved. Twinkle pricked up his ears and yapped excitedly as soon as he spotted his owner. Mandy stroked his head and held him close to her, to stop him from wriggling out of her arms.

'Oof!' James arms were aching. He put Blackie down. 'That's all I can manage,' he groaned.

Mandy waved at Percy, then put Twinkle down too. 'I told Charlie that we'd stop by the grotto with Twinkle,' she said to James.

'Good idea,' said James. 'But I think I'll wait outside with Blackie.'

Mandy nodded. Blackie running around a field was one thing, but putting the lively Labrador in an enclosed space with a table full of raffle prizes was another.

'Hello, Twinkle!' Charlie cuddled the little dog and kissed the top of his head. Twinkle whined softly and licked Charlie's ear. 'Look! He remembers me!' Charlie beamed. 'He's really clever, isn't he?'

Mandy smiled, her hands full of wrapped presents. There wasn't much left to do in the grotto now, although more gifts had been dropped off, and Mandy was just adding these to the pile in front of the display boards.

She glanced at her watch. It was nearly one o'clock, and the bus back to Welford would be leaving soon. 'I have to go now,' she told Charlie. 'I'll bring Twinkle back to see you again if it's OK with Michael.' Charlie stroked Twinkle once more and picked up the end of the lead. As he handed it to Mandy, she saw that he looked rather sad.

'Thanks for bringing him to see me,' he said, managing to smile. Then he brightened up even more. 'I'm all better now. I'm going to be allowed home tomorrow,' he told her proudly.

'That's great news,' Mandy said, but she couldn't help noticing that Charlie's eyes never left Twinkle as she led the little dog out of the grotto. She wondered if Charlie was missing his friend already.

It was two o'clock by the time the bus reached

Welford. Mandy and James got out at the Fox and Goose crossroads, where the smell of roast dinner hung in the air outside the pub.

James sniffed appreciatively. 'Come on, Mandy,' he said. 'Let's take Twinkle home so that we can have our lunch.'

Mandy rolled her eyes. 'I can't believe you're hungry after all those mince-pies!' she teased. But she called to Twinkle and followed James at a brisk pace along the road to Michael's house.

Michael answered the door as soon as they knocked this time. 'Hello again. Did you have a good time?'

'Oh, yes. Twinkle's had a really long walk,' said Mandy. 'And Gran gave us a lift to the hospital so that Percy could see Twinkle again.'

Michael smiled. 'I bet Dad loved that! And I've just had some excellent news. The hospital phoned to say that Dad is making such good progress that he'll be coming home tomorrow.'

'Oh, that's great!' said James.

Mandy handed Twinkle's lead to Michael. The Jack Russell pattered happily into the hallway, looking pleased to be home.

Michael bent down to stroke the little dog. 'I think this little chap has helped Dad get better.

And you've really helped me too. I've managed to get lots of work done today. Thanks very much.'

'That's OK.' Mandy said. 'We enjoyed it – and so did Blackie.'

Michael unclipped Twinkle's lead, then straightened up. 'Dad's going to get a lovely surprise,' he told them. 'My wife and the kids are on their way over from the States. We'll be staying with Dad until the New Year.'

'Percy will love that,' Mandy said. 'And I'll let Gran know. I'm sure she'll have some spare mince-pies for you!'

Michael laughed. 'That would be great!' he said, shutting the door.

As Mandy and James began heading for home, a few snowflakes began to fall. By the time they split up and went their separate ways, the flakes were as big as cottonwool balls, floating down and settling thickly on the icy ground. Blackie looked like a Dalmation in reverse, with big white snowflakes stuck to his shiny black coat.

'A white Christmas after all!' Mandy sang out happily as she turned towards Animal Ark.

Eight

'Laura should be coming in shortly to collect Peaches, Mandy. Would you bring her through when she arrives?' Mrs Hope popped her head round the treatment room door.

'OK,' Mandy said. It was the last surgery before Christmas and she was tidying the magazines in the waiting-room. She had popped into the unit first thing to check on Peaches again. The guinea-pig was lively and alert and ready to go home.

'Would you like to go in now?' Jean Knox sent in the next patient, a woman carrying a pet carrier with a large black cat inside. Then Jean smiled across at Mandy. 'Just this patient for your mum to see, then we can all relax and get on with Christmas.'

Ten minutes later, the woman with the cat came out of the treatment room. She paused by the reception desk as Jean checked her computer, then peeled off a printed label and stuck it on to a small bottle. 'One tablet to be given to Ebony twice a day for a week,' she explained with a smile. The woman took the bottle and thanked Jean. 'Now, do you need to make another appointment?' Jean asked, opening the appointment book.

Mandy glanced up at the clock and felt a tug of anxiety. Laura had better hurry up. It was almost lunch-time and there was no afternoon surgery today.

Suddenly Laura came dashing through the door, followed by her dad. She seemed close to tears. 'Are we too late to pick up Peaches?' she burst out. 'Our car wouldn't start because of the snow. But Dad managed to get it going in the end.'

Mandy smiled warmly. 'Don't worry. You're just in time. I'll take you through, shall I?'

'Phew!' Laura's dad shot Mandy a grateful glance. 'That was close. Without Peaches we'd have had to cancel Christmas!'

'I'll go and get Peaches for you,' Jean offered.

Mandy led the way into the treatment room. While they were waiting for Jean to bring Peaches through from the unit, Emily Hope gave Laura instructions about what to feed her pet from now on. 'Remember, Laura. No plants from the cabbage family, like curly kale and cauliflower. But you can give Peaches small amounts of raw fruit and vegetables for a treat.'

Mandy handed Laura one of the surgery's leaflets about feeding pets. 'This will remind you what she can have if you forget,' she said.

'Thanks, Mandy,' her mum said.

Laura had been listening carefully to Emily Hope. 'No cabbagey stuff,' she repeated seriously. 'What about parsley? It's Peaches's favourite.'

Mrs Hope smiled. 'Parsley's fine.'

'Here we are.' Jean came into the room and put a pet carrier on to the examination table.

'Peaches!' Laura exclaimed, opening the front of the carrier to stroke her beautiful pet. 'Oh, she looks a lot better. Her eyes are all bright.'

'That's because she's feeling well again,' Mandy said. 'I gave her a slice of apple this morning. And she dragged it straight into her nest to eat!'

Laura laughed. 'She always does that. She must

be feeling like her old self.'

'She's recovered really well considering her age,' Emily Hope agreed.

Laura stroked Peaches gently. 'Dad's built you a hayrack to fix to the side of your hutch, so you won't tread on your food,' she whispered to her pet. Peaches looked up at her with beady black eyes and twitched her nose.

'It sounds like Peaches is going to get four-star treatment then,' Mrs Hope said.

'Well, we know what she's getting for Christmas dinner,' Mandy joked. 'Parsley!'

Laura picked Peaches up and placed her carefully in the cardboard pet carrier. Her dad carried it out of the treatment room and stood at Jean's desk while he settled the bill. Then Mandy held the door for them and waved to Laura as she got into her dad's car. After they had left, Mandy helped lock up the surgery. Jean Knox put her coat and scarf on and picked up her handbag.

Mandy put her hand in the pocket of her fleece and took out a small, flat parcel. 'Happy Christmas, Jean,' she said.

'Oh, thank you dear,' Jean said, beaming. She took the parcel and popped in into her bag. 'Happy Christmas to you too. And you might find a little something from me under your Christmas tree!'

'That was kind of you,' Emily Hope said after Jean had gone. 'What was in the parcel?'

'Oh, just a new chain for Jean's glasses,' Mandy answered with a grin. 'So she's got a spare in case she loses her other one!'

'Just time for lunch before I face my public!' Adam Hope said, tucking into a pile of sandwiches. He looked longingly at Gran's mince-pies.

'No time for pudding.' Emily Hope grinned at her husband. 'Your grotto is ready and waiting.'

'Da-ad! You won't fit in your Santa suit if you carry on eating like that!' Mandy joked. Now that the last surgery was over, she was tingling with excitement. It felt as if Christmas had started already.

'But it's Christmas Eve!' her dad pointed out. He reached out and took a warm mince-pie. 'Mmm. Lovely. I think I'll go and clear the drive. Might work that little lot off!' He wiped his mouth and headed out of the back door.

'I'll fetch your Santa suit,' Mandy volunteered. She went into the sitting-room where the outfit was hanging, and carried the fake-fur trimmed red suit into the kitchen. Suddenly a yell rang out. Mandy froze. That sounded like her dad's voice. She dashed out to the drive, where Mr Hope had dropped the yard brush on to the snow. Emily Hope was there already, helping Mandy's dad move gingerly towards the house.

'What's happened?' Mandy burst out.

Adam Hope winced with pain. 'It's my back,' he groaned. 'I slipped on a patch of ice – I think I've strained it.'

'Oh, no! We're supposed to be leaving for the hospital in a minute,' Mandy said.

'Your dad won't be coming, I'm afraid,' Emily Hope said firmly. 'He can't possibly be Santa now.' She turned to her husband. 'Remember when you strained your back before, Adam?'

'Yes,' her husband murmured, rubbing his back. 'I couldn't sit down for a week! I'm sorry Mandy, love. I really hate to let everyone down. But I just can't do it.'

Mandy's heart sank. She thought of all the children who were looking forward to visiting Santa in the grotto. This was a total disaster!

Once they were all back in the kitchen, Emily Hope took a packet of painkillers out of the cupboard and filled a glass with water. Mandy's

dad swallowed the pills, then limped out of the room, heading for the sitting-room.

'I'm going to lie on the floor,' he told them through clenched teeth.

Mandy sat down at the table and propped her chin on her hand. 'Now what are we going to do?' she wailed.

Emily Hope raised her eyebrows. 'OK. Let's not panic. But we do need to find another Santa – and quickly!'

'What about Grandad?' Mandy began. Then her face fell. 'Oh, I've just remembered. He's taking mince-pies and Christmas puddings to Gran's Meals-on-Wheels people.'

That's right,' her mum confirmed. 'Your gran's at the hospital this afternoon, so she couldn't do it herself.'

'There's no time left to ask anyone else, is there?' Mandy said glumly. She felt defeated. This was too awful.

'Maybe we could hand out the presents ourselves?' Emily Hope suggested.

'Mu-um!' Mandy looked at her mum aghast. 'Not without Santa!' She stared out the kitchen window, racking her brain for a Santa substitute. Then she jumped up from the table. 'Wait a minute. I've just thought of someone who might do it. Come on!'

Snow blew thickly against the windscreen as Emily Hope drove the Land-rover carefully up the winding road across the moors. The fields and hedgerows were carpeted with a thick white blanket, and the snow formed smoky, wave-shaped drifts as the wind blew it against the walls.

As soon as they drew into the hospital car park, Mandy jumped out and raced into the invitingly warm building. She was gasping for breath by the time she reached Ward Twelve. Gran and Percy were standing by Percy's bed. The old man was dressed in a thick coat and muffler and had a tweed cap on his head. It looked as though Percy was just about to go home.

Gran looked up in alarm as Mandy rushed to the bedside. 'What's the matter? Has something happened?'

'It's Dad!' Mandy managed to gasp. 'He's slipped and strained his back. He's OK, but he can't sit down, so he can't be Santa now. We need to find someone else to do it!'

'Oh dear,' Gran said. She glanced at her watch. 'But it's too late. The children will start arriving in about twenty minutes.'

'I know!' Mandy said. She took a deep breath. Would she be able to persuade Percy to step in? She remembered her gran saying that Percy was a very private person, but this was an emergency...

But Percy was already taking off his cap and muffler. He unbuttoned his heavy outdoor coat. 'I'll do it,' he said. 'Lead me to the Santa suit. I've heard so much about this grotto, I'd love to see it.'

'Oh, Percy! Thank you!' Mandy exclaimed. Without thinking, she stood on tiptoe and gave his wrinkled cheek a kiss. 'The suit's still in the car. I'll go and bring it in . . .'

'Hold your horses a minute, Mandy love,' Gran interrupted. 'Percy has been quite poorly. This might be too much for him.'

'Oh.' Mandy hadn't thought of that. Her shoulders sagged.

But Percy spoke up. 'Now don't you worry about me. I feel fine,' he protested.

Gran nodded, smiling. 'I'm sure you do, Percy. But I think you should check with a doctor first, just to be on the safe side.'

Percy winked at Mandy. 'All right, Dorothy. If

that will set your mind at rest.'

'It would.' Gran was unmoving.

Mandy's patience felt stretched to the limit. She knew that her gran was right, but there were only fifteen minutes left now before the visitors began arriving. She fidgeted anxiously as she watched the seconds tick past on her watch. Just then, Sister Lacey entered the ward, followed by a tall blond man in a white coat. 'Here's the doctor now,' said Gran.

'I'll go and have a word with him.' Percy left his coat on the chair and went over.

Mandy waited tensely beside Gran. What were they going to do if the doctor decided that Percy ought to go straight home and rest?

Percy beamed as he came back over to Gran and Mandy. 'I've got the all-clear! The doctor thinks being Santa is a great idea. Especially as I will be sitting down anyway for most of the time.'

'Fantastic!' Mandy didn't need telling twice. 'I'll meet you and Gran at the grotto!' She sped away to tell her mum the good news and fetch the Santa suit.

'Ho ho ho!' Percy had put on the Santa suit and was trying out his hearty Santa laugh. The suit was a bit long for him, but the rich scarlet clothes looked very festive. He had even hooked Adam Hope's fake white beard over his ears, although it tended to slip off if he moved his head too quickly.

Percy sat on a comfortable armchair borrowed from Sister Lacey's office. Next to him was a sack, bulging with toys from the Christmas appeal, all wrapped in brightly-coloured paper.

'You look great, Percy,' Mandy told him.

'Very Christmassy,' agreed Gran, putting a cushion behind Percy's back. 'But you're to stop at once if you start feeling tired, do you hear?'

Percy grinned at Mandy. 'Merry Christmas everyone!' he boomed. His pale blue eyes sparkled and his cheeks were a healthy pink above the thick white beard.

'Dad? Is that you?' said a surprised voice.

Mandy turned and saw that Michael had come into the grotto room. Twinkle stood beside him, his ears pricked up and his head on one side as he studied the Santa figure.

'I've just been into the ward and the nurse told me you were in here,' Michael said. 'But I didn't expect this!'

'Hello, son. Come to visit Santa have you?' Percy joked. 'And what do you want for Christmas?'

Mandy chuckled. Percy was a great Santa.

'I've had my present, thanks,' Michael said warmly. 'My dad's going to be home and well for Christmas.'

Mandy went over and gave Twinkle a cuddle. 'Hello again, boy. Come to say hello to Percy, have you?'

Twinkle whined softly. He sat down and held up one paw, inviting Mandy to shake hands.

'Well, I never,' Percy said. 'He's never done that before!'

'Charlie must have taught him,' Mandy said.

Gran nodded. 'That lad's been brilliant with Twinkle,' she remarked.

Mandy took Twinkle's paw and gave it a gentle shake. 'This is perfect!' she said. 'We've haven't just got a new Santa – we've got his honorary reindeer here too!'

Twinkle gave a short bark and his tail whipped about madly. He obviously agreed.

Nine

On the dot of three o'clock, children began coming into the grotto. Many of them were in dressing-gowns and slippers and some had nurses or parents accompanying them.

'Shall we get your reindeer dressed?' Mandy suggested to Percy.

'Eh? Oh, you mean the antlers Charlie made.' Percy grinned. 'He told me all about them. I can't wait to see Twinkle wearing them.'

Mandy found the antlers behind the display boards and tied them on. Twinkle shook his head a couple of times, but he seemed pleased to be wearing his antlers again.

'There. You do look smart!' Mandy told him admiringly.

Just then James arrived. 'Hi! Sorry I'm a bit late. The road across the moors is blocked, so we had to go through the valley.' He glanced over to where Santa was surrounded by children. 'Your dad's doing a great job,' he said to Mandy.

'My dad?' Mandy laughed. 'Look again!'

James peered across the crowded grotto. Santa was leaning down to listen as the children told him what they wanted for Christmas. His false beard had slipped to one side a bit.

James frowned. 'That's not your Dad! It looks like . . .'

'Percy? Yes – it is him!' said Mandy. 'Dad slipped on some ice and hurt his back, so Percy stepped in.'

'And he's having the time of his life,' Michael said. 'I haven't seen Dad look this happy since the day I brought Twinkle home for him.'

Mandy had to agree. The frail, depressed old man had gone, and now Percy looked cheerful and confident as he chatted to his eager visitors.

Twinkle lay at Percy's feet, snuffling contentedly through a pile of loose tinsel. His antlers bobbed and wobbled as he dug his nose into the glittery strands, and sneezed when they tickled his nose.

James nudged Mandy. 'I think Twinkle's enjoying himself, too!' he said.

Mandy grinned. 'A terrier in the tinsel! What a perfect Christmas present for Percy – he's going home and back to Twinkle.' At the sound of his name, the Jack Russell looked up and barked, but he didn't move from Percy's feet.

Michael turned to Mandy and James. 'As Dad seems to be tied up for a while, I'm just going to nip out and do some last-minute shopping.'

'OK,' Mandy said. 'We'll look after Twinkle, don't worry.'

'Oh, I almost forgot. Just before I go . . .' Michael went and whispered something in Percy's ear.

Then Mandy saw him take a bulky wrapped parcel from his overcoat pocket and slip it into Santa's sack. Percy gave a secret smile and nodded at his son.

Strange, Mandy thought. Who was that special gift for?

'Cool! Twinkle's here!' Charlie bounded into the grotto wearing jeans, a thick jumper and trainers.

'Hi, Charlie,' called James.

'I thought you were going home today,' Mandy said.

'I am,' Charlie replied promptly. 'Mum's coming to fetch me. But I wanted to see Santa before I go.' 'Specially as the nurse told me it's Percy. I've got a present for him.'

'What is it?' Mandy asked curiously.

But Charlie wasn't telling. 'Wait and see!' he teased. While Charlie was waiting his turn, he went over to see Twinkle. Twinkle immediately rolled on to his back, inviting Charlie to stroke his pale tummy. Charlie giggled and tickled him.

The grotto seemed to be getting even busier. The display boards swayed perilously as more children crowded in to see Santa. Mandy's gran was at the door taking money from the children who weren't in hospital, and already her plastic money tub was encouragingly full.

'You go and help Percy give out the presents,' James suggested, 'and I'll help your gran. That queue out there is getting a bit unruly!' He marched out of the grotto, and Mandy heard him asking the waiting children to line up on one side of the corridor. Mandy wriggled through the people and made her way behind the raffle table, to Percy's side. She picked up a slippery armful of presents and got ready to hand them out.

It was Charlie's turn to see Santa. Mandy thought he looked rather shy, all of a sudden. He was holding a long, tube-shaped gift.

Percy bent down and beamed through his beard. 'Hello, young man,' he said.

'Hello, Santa,' Charlie answered. He thrust the present towards Percy. 'This is for you.'

'For me?' Percy sounded surprised. 'What's all this, eh? Santa's supposed to give you a present, not the other way round!'

'It's a special one. You can open it now,' Charlie said seriously. 'You don't have to wait until Christmas Day.'

'In that case, I will!' Percy opened his present. It was a large, rolled-up sheet of paper. As Percy unrolled, it his eyes widened. 'That's grand!' he exclaimed.

Mandy leaned over his shoulder to look. It was a portrait of Twinkle. The little dog was sitting in a heap of red tinsel, with his head cocked on one side. One strand hung round his neck. Charlie had even captured the cheeky glint in the little dog's eye.

'It's brilliant!' Mandy gasped. 'Really life-like!'

'Did you paint that, Charlie?' James peered

across the room and called over to them. 'It's fantastic.'

'It certainly is,' Percy echoed. 'It's grand, Charlie,' he repeated. 'Best present I've ever had!'

Charlie's face was bright pink, but he looked really pleased. Twinkle jumped up and pawed at Charlie's jeans. He barked as if in approval.

Percy grinned. 'There you are. Twinkle agrees with me!' Percy rolled up the painting again and stored it safely under his chair. Then he adjusted his false beard and smoothed down his red Santa suit. 'Now it's your turn, Charlie. What would you like for Christmas?' he asked.

Charlie beamed. He leaned close and spoke quietly so that only Percy and Mandy could hear. 'What I'd really like is my very own dog. Just like Twinkle.'

Mandy felt a pang of sympathy. But while Charlie and his mum live in a flat, and are out all day, she knew it just wasn't practical. There was just no way he could have a pet dog.

Just then, Mandy heard a commotion in the corridor. James appeared in the doorway, looking rather flustered.

'I can assure you, my dear, that my dogs are clean, healthy and obedient!' The plummy voice floated into the grotto room. 'I can vouch for them personally.'

Mandy raised her eyebrows at James. Mrs Ponsonby!'

'I'm afraid I'll have to get permission from the ward sister before you bring in your dogs . . .' One of the nurses was explaining patiently.

'But I'm Amelia Ponsonby from Bleakfell Hall,' Mrs Ponsonby interrupted. 'Ah, here's someone who'll vouch for me. Dorothy, dear, would you just . . .'

The conversation outside subsided into a murmur. James busied himself at the door, taking money from some waiting children. Mandy straightened the gifts on the raffle table.

A few moments later, Mrs Ponsonby swept into the room. She wore a smart purple coat and a matching woolly hat. Pandora was tucked under her arm and Toby trotted on a lead by her side. Both dogs wore smart little coats.

'Well – really! I only wanted to pop into the grotto for a few minutes,' Mrs Ponsonby blustered to Gran, who was hovering behind her.

'I expect it's hospital policy for everyone to get permission to bring in a dog, Amelia,' Gran said hastily.

'You're probably right,' Mrs Ponsonby tailed off as she surveyed the grotto. Her eyes flicked over the silver pillars, the foil-covered walls with their tinsel streamers and stars, and Santa sitting on his comfortable armchair. 'This is all splendid!' she boomed, looking up at Charlie's banner. 'My, you have all worked hard.' She marched over to the raffle table and started inspecting the prizes.

Toby trotted over to Twinkle. The two dogs sniffed each other curiously, their ears pricked. Then Toby bounced down low on to his front paws, inviting Twinkle to play. Twinkle leaped up and lunged forward, yapping playfully. Toby darted sideways, whipped round, and took off across the grotto.

Mandy laughed. Twinkle had completely forgotten that he was supposed to be an honorary reindeer! As he bowled into Toby, his antlers were knocked sideways and hung limply over his shoulder.

Toby sprang up and pretended to nip Twinkle's ear. Twinkle growled with mock fierceness and scampered behind Percy's armchair. His tiny claws ticked against the hard floor. In a second, Twinkle reappeared with a trailing end of tinsel in his mouth. He shook his head, worrying it like a rat.

Toby seemed very excited by the shiny stuff. He grabbed the other end of it and backed off, a growl rumbling cheerfully in his throat.

'Cool! A tug-of-war!' Charlie stood at the edge of the room and watched the dogs pulling the tinsel, until it was stretched out between them.

Twinkle and Toby edged sideways, closer and closer to Mrs Ponsonby. Then Toby leaped forward, still holding the tinsel. As Twinkle swerved away, the tinsel streamer became wound round the old lady's sturdy ankles. It was pulled steadily tighter as the dogs dodged around her.

'Oh, my goodness! I can't move! Someone help me!' Mrs Ponsonby boomed dramatically.

Mandy felt laughter bubbling up inside her as she ran over and grabbed Toby. Charlie managed to catch Twinkle and knelt down beside him, holding him still. The little dog looked up at him, panting, with his pink tongue lolling out. He still seemed raring to go. James sprang forward and helped to unravel the tinsel from Mrs Ponsonby's ankles.

Mrs Ponsonby stamped her feet impatiently. 'Do hurry and get it off, James dear! It's upsetting poor Pandora!'

Pandora blinked placidly, eyeing James calmly from her place in Mrs Ponsonby's arms.

Keeping one hand on Toby's collar, Mandy rolled up the tinsel streamer. She stuffed it into her pocket, so there was no chance of Twinkle running off with it again!

As soon as her feet were free, Mrs Ponsonby clipped Toby's lead on and swept out of the grotto in a flurry of purple coat and strong perfume. 'I'll be back to see you later, Dorothy,' she promised Mandy's gran threateningly. 'When that disobedient terrier has gone!'

'Oh dear.' Percy looked a bit worried. 'Twinkle's

being a bit of a handful, isn't he? I hope he's not going to misbehave again.'

'I'll look after him until Mum gets here if you like,' Charlie offered. He was still kneeling on the floor, stroking Twinkle's back.

'Thanks, lad,' Percy said gratefully.

Twinkle looked up at Charlie, then put his chin on his front paws, as if he understood that the game had finished.

'He really has a way with dogs, hasn't he?' Gran had been watching Charlie keep Twinkle under control.

'Yes,' James agreed. 'Twinkle and Charlie have really taken to each other.' He took a pound coin from the last person in the queue and led them to Santa's armchair. Mandy took another toy out of Santa's sack and passed it to Percy. The little girl took it from Santa with a delighted grin and ran off to show it to her mum, who was waiting by the door.

Mandy heaved a sigh of relief and propped herself on the edge of the raffle table. Galloping footsteps out in the corridor made Mandy look up. Charlie was racing up and down with Twinkle bounding at his heels, full of energy, as usual. Then Mandy looked at Percy. The old man looked tired and little pale, and his breath sounded a bit noisy. Suddenly the beginnings of a brilliant idea crept into Mandy's mind.

'Twinkle's so cheeky and lively, isn't he?' she began. 'It looks like you could do with some help with him.'

'Mandy's right, Percy,' Gran agreed, coming over with the tub of money. 'It's going to be some time before you're completely better. And as we've seen, Twinkle needs rather a lot of attention.'

Percy's head came up. He looked a bit uncomfortable. 'Thanks, but I can manage,' he said shortly. 'I don't want anyone coming along and taking Twinkle away because they think he's too much for me!'

Mandy's heart sank. Now Percy was upset. This wasn't meant to happen. How on earth was she going to get him to agree to her perfect solution?

Ten

Mandy took a deep breath. She decided to try again. 'Actually, Percy,' she began carefully. 'I was just thinking. What about if Charlie helped you with Twinkle?'

Percy turned towards her. He still looked a bit ruffled. 'How do you mean?'

'Well, you know how much Charlie loves dogs, especially Twinkle? And he can't have one of his own because he lives in a flat and his mum works all day,' Mandy rushed on, warming to her theme. James nodded eagerly to support her. 'I bet he'd jump at the chance to come and take Twinkle out for walks. And you would be making his dream

come true if you let him see Twinkle
sometimes . . .' Mandy caught Gran's eye. She was
looking rather stern. Mandy paused. Would Percy
agree? He seemed so determined to be
independent. Beside her, James held his breath.

Suddenly Percy's face cleared. 'Oh, right,' he
said slowly. 'So I'd still *keep* Twinkle. Charlie would
just be helping me out, as it were?'

'That's it!' said Mandy eagerly. 'He could take
Twinkle out for walks, and you'd be able to get
better more quickly.

Percy looked thoughtful. 'Well, I suppose he
could give it a go,' he said at last.

Just then, Charlie popped his head in the door.
'Hi Mandy!' he called. 'Did you see how fast
Twinkle can run?'

'Yes, I did,' said Mandy. 'And Charlie, Percy has
just said that you can come and see Twinkle again,
when he's at home.'

Charlie's face lit up. He ran over to Percy's chair.
'Can I, Mr Green? Can I come and visit Twinkle
and take him for walks?'

'Course you can, lad,' Percy said, patting Charlie
on the shoulder. 'I'd like nothing better.'

'Oh, that's great!' Charlie exclaimed.

Percy looked subdued for a moment. 'If I'm

honest, my legs aren't quite what they used to be. I'm not really up to taking Twinkle for a good long walk every day.'

'But I am!' Charlie told him happily. 'And you can tell me more about dog breeding and terrier racing too. Because I'm definitely going to work with dogs when I grow up.'

Percy chuckled at Charlie's enthusiasm. 'I reckon you will too. I was dog mad just like you when I was a nipper!'

Charlie bent down and wrapped his arms round Twinkle. The little dog jumped up and balanced his front paws on Charlie's knee. Then he reached upward and licked his face. 'We're going to have such fun together, Twinkle,' Charlie promised. 'Just wait until I tell Mum about you.'

'I'm afraid I've heard enough, Charlie,' said a voice behind them.

Mandy and James turned round to see Linda Kingston. She had come to collect Charlie and was holding her son's outdoor clothes over her arm.

'Hi, Mrs Kingston,' Mandy said. She hopped down from the table and walked across to greet her.

But Linda Kingston was looking down at

Charlie cuddling Twinkle. Her mouth was set in a stern line. 'Now, Charlie,' she said firmly, 'I've told you that you can't have a dog. It's no use you trying to persuade me yet again.'

James and Mandy glanced at each other in alarm.

'But I'm not, Mum!' Charlie interrupted, looking hurt. 'I know you're going to love Twinkle . . .'

'That's enough, Charlie!' Mrs Kingston said in an annoyed voice. She looked at Mandy and James and frowned. 'I'm afraid you really mustn't encourage Charlie to think he can have a dog. Especially when I've explained the situation to you both.'

'But we haven't, have we, James?' Mandy said hurriedly, going a bit pink.

James shook his head vigorously. 'Charlie doesn't want to keep Twinkle,' he explained. 'He just wants to help Percy look after him.'

Mrs Kingston looked at Charlie. 'Is this true?' she asked, her face clearing.

Charlie rolled his eyes. 'Yes! That's what I've been trying to tell you! Twinkle is still Percy's dog, not mine!'

Then Percy spoke up. 'You've got a fine lad

there, Mrs Kingston. He's been brilliant with my Twinkle these past few days. He's really cheered me up, I can tell you. And he's drawn me a wonderful picture of Twinkle for Christmas. Now he's offered to come and take him for walks to save my old legs. You should be proud of him.'

Mandy and James exchanged hopeful glances.

Mrs Kingston looked at Charlie and Percy, then down at Twinkle. 'Oh dear. I've been jumping to conclusions, haven't I?' She turned to Mandy and James. 'I think I owe you both an apology.'

'That's all right,' Mandy said quickly.

'So – you don't mind me helping out with Twinkle then?' Charlie said to his mum.

Mrs Kingston shook her head. 'Mind? I think it's wonderful!' She put a hand on her son's shoulder. 'The doctor said you needed to get plenty of fresh air and exercise. And I can't imagine a little dog like that is going to tire you out much.'

Mandy opened her mouth to protest, but James nudged her and she shut it again. Out of the corner of her eye, she saw Percy wink at her.

Charlie beamed. He gave Twinkle another cuddle. 'I'm going to come and take you out every day after school,' he whispered into his soft brown ear. 'And in school holidays we can go for super-long walks over the fields. This is the best Christmas present I've ever had!'

Percy gave a chuckle. 'Well, I am Santa, after all!' he declared, his blue eyes twinkling.

It was time for Santa to do a tour of the children's ward. He was going to meet the children who were too poorly to leave their beds and visit the grotto. Mandy was a bit worried that Percy would be tired by now, but he insisted he felt fine. Gran brought him a cup of tea and encouraged him to have a rest as they packed up the presents.

'There have been so many donations of toys this year,' Mandy said, as she picked up a bulging sack.

'I think some people came back twice, just to see Twinkle!' James joked.

Sister Lacey had given permission for Twinkle to do the round with Percy. His antlers were fixed firmly in place. Before he went home with his mum, Charlie had woven a strip of tinsel around Twinkle's collar. The terrier looked very festive, and trotted eagerly around their feet, sniffing at the sacks of presents.

Mandy and James shouldered a sack of toys

each. To make them look more festive, Gran had produced two elves' hats made of green felt, with a bell on the pointed end. Mandy hoped they weren't going to pass any mirrors – she didn't think James would keep his hat on if he knew how funny he looked!

'Everyone ready? Let's go!' Percy started forward, followed by his honorary reindeer and two elf helpers.

Just before they entered the children's ward, James made them all stop. 'Hang on a minute everyone!' he said. 'I nearly forgot.' He delved into his trouser pocket and produced a CD. Dashing across to the ward sister, he asked her if she would play it for them. Then he hurried back to join Mandy, Percy and Twinkle. 'OK!' he said. 'We're ready!'

'What's on the CD?' Mandy asked.

'Oh, just Christmas carols,' James replied. Then he lowered his voice. 'And there's a surprise at the end for Percy,' he whispered.

As Santa stepped through the doorway into the ward, the strains of 'Hark! the Herald Angels Sing' rang out.

'Ho ho ho! Merry Christmas everyone!' Percy's cheery voice filled the ward.

Twinkle trotted along beside Percy, his head held high and his tail wagging furiously. His glittery tinsel collar shone and his antlers stood up perkily. He gave a couple of excited barks.

'I think he's saying Happy Christmas too!' Mandy said.

'Oh, look at that funny dog!' said a little boy in a blue dressing-gown. He wriggled to the end of his bed for a closer look.

'Isn't he gorgeous!' agreed his mum. She reached down and patted Twinkle, who had come up to say hello.

Percy sat down at the bedside of a pale little girl who looked about six years old. Her mum and dad sat with her. Mandy hovered at the end of the bed, carrying the sack of presents.

'Hello there. Merry Christmas! And what's your name?' Percy asked in a friendly voice.

'Fiona,' the little girl told him shyly. She was propped up against a bank of pillows. 'Is that your dog?' she asked, leaning over to look at Twinkle, who had scampered across the ward to join them.

Percy nodded. 'He's my special helper. He's called Twinkle.'

'Can I stroke him?' asked the little girl.

'Course you can,' said Mandy. She put down her sack and lifted Twinkle up so that Fiona could reach him. Fiona's parents looked a bit concerned, as if they thought Twinkle might be a bit too lively for their sick daughter.

But Twinkle snuggled down in Mandy's arms and whined softly in a friendly fashion while he was stroked. The little girl's face lit up, and she beamed proudly at her mum and dad as Twinkle nudged his head against her hand, asking for more attention. Percy took a pink-wrapped gift from the sack and laid it on the bed.

More Christmas carols rang out as they moved down the ward. Now it was 'Once in Royal David's City'.

Most of the other children were just as eager to make a fuss of the little dog. Mandy and James took turns in picking Twinkle up and holding him while his ears were ruffled and his coat was stroked over and over.

Twinkle behaved perfectly. He didn't even seem to mind when one of the children bent down and whispered into his ear.

'That must tickle!' Mandy said to James.

'He seems to know he has to be gentle, doesn't he?' James agreed.

Percy was a brilliant Santa. He spoke to every child, giving them presents and asking them what they wanted for Christmas. Mandy felt very proud as she watched the children excitedly opening their presents.

'Wow! A giant book of animal stories!' A boy with his leg in plaster showed his present to his smiling parents.

At last every patient had been visited. Santa waved as he began to make his way back up the ward. 'Goodbye everyone. Have a wonderful Christmas!' Percy called.

The last carol ended. There was a pause, then a familiar tune started up. 'Twinkle, Twinkle, Little Star!'

'It's Twinkle's song!' Mandy said with a laugh. So *that* was James's surprise.

Percy beamed, and walked slowly out of the ward with Twinkle bouncing at his heels. He led the way back to the grotto, where they began to tidy up. The ice cave had started to look rather tatty, and there were stray bits of tinsel and torn wrapping paper everywhere.

'Oh, what's this?' Mandy shook her sack. 'There's something left in the bottom.'

Percy reached into the sack and took out a

wrapped parcel. He smiled at James. 'I think this is for you.'

'It can't be.' James looked blank as he took hold of the parcel. 'I'm not in hospital.'

'It's got your name on the label.' Percy insisted.

'To Blackie care of James Hunter – best wishes from Twinkle,' James read aloud. He looked at Mandy. 'Do you know what it is?'

Mandy shook her head. 'Why don't you open it and find out?' she suggested. She watched curiously as James tore open the wrapper.

He looked into the parcel, and let out a burst

of laughter. He grinned at Mandy and held up a doggy Christmas stocking.

'That's to replace the one you donated to Twinkle!' Percy told him.

The stocking was enormous. Even bigger than the one Twinkle had eaten. There were bags of dog treats, dog chews, dog shampoo, and even a smart new collar.

'It's fantastic. Blackie's going to love this,' James said happily. 'Thank you, Percy.'

Mandy smiled to herself. So that's what Michael had been whispering to his dad about!

Just then, Sister Lacey popped her head round the door and offered them the use of her office, so that Percy could take off his Santa suit. Mandy and James went with him to give him a hand. The old man seemed tired but Mandy could see that the was glowing with happiness.

'Thanks so much, Percy. You were a brilliant Santa,' she said to him.

Percy smiled at her. 'I really enjoyed myself, lass. And so did Twinkle!'

As if in response, Twinkle gave a short answering bark.

'I think Twinkle was even more popular than Santa!' James joked.

'Quite right too!' Percy grinned. That was fine by him. He was very proud of his clever, friendly dog.

Suddenly a group of people appeared at the doorway. 'Surprise!'

It was Michael, with his wife and two small children – all just arrived from the States. Twinkle raced over to meet them, his tail wagging madly.

Percy stood stock still. His tired face lit up with a huge smile. 'Well, I never,' he breathed delightedly.

'Merry Christmas, Grandad!' chorused his family.

'Come on, let's leave them to it,' Mandy whispered to James. 'Gran will be waiting for us.'

They crept out of Sister Lacey's office, and took one last look at the excited scene. Percy was sitting down with an arm round each of his grandchildren. Twinkle stood beside him with his front paws on Percy's knees, licking anyone who came within reach.

Mandy smiled. 'That's the best present,' she said to James. 'Percy's got all his family with him for Christmas.

'And don't forget Charlie's got a share in

Twinkle,' James reminded her. 'I bet he can't wait to see him again!'

'That's right,' said Mandy. 'Twinkle's been a real Santa's helper this year!'

Another Hodder Children's book

POLARS ON THE PATH
Animal Ark 53

Lucy Daniels

Mandy Hope is having an Arctic adventure! She can't wait to meet the amazing animals that live amongst the snow and ice.

The Hopes are in the small town of Churchill to watch polar bears migrating north. It's a spectacular sight. But when one of the cubs strays from his mother, Mandy fears for its safety. Can she help reunite the cub with his family before winter sets in?